"I don't like being followed. Or manipulated. Or being treated like some fragile little girl who can't take care of herself," Danielle said.

"Poor little rich girl." Jake didn't bother masking the contempt in his voice. He wondered what she'd think of the way he'd grown up, fighting his way out of the slums with nothing but his fists and a fierce determination to make a better life for himself and his sister.

Her head jerked up. He could see her rebuild a mask of composure. "Think what you want."

The words were said with a studied lack of concern, but he heard the pain behind them. He had no desire to hurt her, but he wasn't willing to back down from doing his job.

"I have a job to do," he said, as though to reinforce his thoughts...and his resolve. "It'll be a lot easier if you cooperate. But I'm here to stay." To prove his point, Jake cupped her elbow and steered her to his Jeep.

"Have it your way."

"I usually do."

JANE M. CHOATE

dreamed of writing from the time she was a small child when she used to entertain her friends with made-up stories. Her true writing career began when she penned a story for a children's magazine, sent it in on a whim and found, to her delight, that it was accepted. She was hooked. Someone was paying her to write! Writing for the Harlequin Love Inspired Suspense line is a dream come true. Jane is the proud mother of five children, grandmother to four grandchildren and the staff to one cat who believes she is of royal descent.

KEEPING WATCH

JANE M. CHOATE

HARLEQUIN® LOVE INSPIRED® SUSPENSE

Recycling programs
for this product may
not exist in your area.

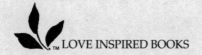 LOVE INSPIRED BOOKS

ISBN-13: 978-0-373-44629-2

KEEPING WATCH

www.Harlequin.com

Printed in U.S.A.

They should see with their eyes, and hear with their ears, and should understand with their heart, and should be converted, and I should heal them.
—*Matthew* 13:15

To Tina James, who took a chance on me.

And

Amanda Cabot, who saw me through revisions, obsessions and neuroses. She is truly a sister of the heart.

ONE

Danielle Barclay moved quickly, always in a rush to keep up with her own ambitions. Today, though, she hurried for a different reason: someone was following her. She couldn't shake the feeling, not even now when she was the only passenger in the elevator on her way to the fourteenth floor of the county building. Fear whispered up her spine.

Hurry. Hurry.

The gold script on her office door, Danielle Barclay, Deputy District Attorney, never failed to elicit a spurt of pride in her, but today she was feeling too unsettled to appreciate it. That this was the four-year anniversary of her mother's disappearance didn't help matters any. Her mind flinched at the memories.

When she passed her secretary's desk, Clariss said, "Ms. Barclay, there's a package on your desk."

Danielle nodded in response, her mind elsewhere. Another anonymous note had arrived in yesterday's mail. Though the threats had been vague, she didn't discount the potential seriousness of the situation.

Her gaze landed on the package. It bore the distinctive wrapping paper of her favorite store. A peace offering, she thought, from her father. Guilt pressed the back of her neck as she remembered the last time they had talked. Things had been tense between them for the past two weeks, ever since the first threatening letter had arrived. A shiver skittered down her spine as she recalled the words: "You will pay for your sins."

Foolishly, she'd told her father about it.

In retrospect, she wished she had kept it to herself. Senator Stewart Barclay had acted predictably, insisting that she move back home under his watchful eye and that of his security staff.

Her relationship with her father had frequently been difficult, an emotional tug-of-war she always lost precisely because she loved him. Not this time, she thought. Not this time. She would handle the stalking on her own.

She thrust those disturbing thoughts from her mind, promising herself she'd deal with the package later. Right now, she had seven cases pending. She didn't need another distraction, not when her mind was already weighed down with worry.

Only when she settled behind the desk in her office did her brain unlock. Only then did she break free of the obsessive loop of fears that persisted in playing in her head. Of course she wasn't being followed. Her imagination had taken root and gone wild. Slowly, she let the clogged air out of her lungs.

It was here, in her office, that she could occasionally not think about her mother for hours at a time and thus force the uncertainty of what had happened to her to retreat into her subconscious. She knew that wouldn't be the case today.

Still, work was the best antidote for worry, she knew, so she started drafting a brief. Four hours later, when her stomach rumbled, a reminder that she hadn't taken the time to eat any breakfast, her gaze once again landed on the package.

With a sigh, she opened it. A sour smell assaulted her nostrils, and she gasped.

A gutted fish lay nestled among the layers of tissue paper. Decomposing entrails made it a particularly gruesome sight. With trembling fingers, she picked up the note that accompanied the hideous gift.

Unable to help herself, she read the words aloud. "'Roses are red. Violets are blue. This fish is dead, and so are you.'"

She dropped the note, realizing it could bear fingerprints. Although, thus far none of the letters she'd received had prints.

Eyes closed, Dani, a nickname her mother had given her, felt the sting of tears behind them. She clenched her arms around her ribs in an effort to keep herself from shaking. For seven years, she'd fought for her place in the Fulton County District Attorney's Office. She was making her mark in Atlanta her own way, in her own time. If some lowlife thought he could scare her away, he was mistaken.

A soft prayer passed through her lips. "Lord, I can't handle this on my own. I need You. Please share Your strength with me." Turning to the Lord when she needed help was as instinctive as breathing. At once, she felt stronger, more in control.

"Enough," she said, whether to her stalker or herself, she wasn't sure. She picked up the phone, punched in a single number and said, "Clariss, would you come in here, please?"

Within seconds, her secretary appeared. "Oh, I see you opened…" Her gaze landed on the contents of the package. "Is that some kind of joke?"

"Not a very good one," Dani said. "Did you know how this…thing got here?"

Clariss shook her head. "It was here when I arrived this morning."

Dani nodded, not expecting anything different. But how had whoever had left the hideous thing gotten inside her office? During nonworking hours, it was never left unlocked. The city building where the D.A.'s offices were located was constantly patrolled and checked by night watchmen.

"Please call Detective Monroe and ask him to send someone to pick this up." Jeff Monroe, assigned to the

D.A.'s office, had been following up on the letters and calls she'd received.

She recognized the enormity of his task. With seven cases pending and the dozens of others she'd prosecuted over the years, the list of those with a reason to wish her harm was a very long one. Too long.

"Right away, Ms. Barclay."

"It's Dani. And thanks."

Clariss was just out of college and persisted in addressing her as "Ms. Barclay." Now Clariss smiled, softening her usually hardened face.

Dani gazed at the offending package, the awful note, and barely repressed a shudder. She couldn't work here, not with that thing staring at her, and she wasn't about to waste a day, so she decided to interview a witness for an upcoming case. She picked up her purse and headed for the door.

"You can reach me on my cell if you need me," she told Clariss. "I'm going to be in the field."

An hour later, Dani was ready to admit defeat.

The witness had proved not only uncooperative but was now recanting her account of what had transpired. Dani did her best to remind the woman of her earlier statement, only to have her become belligerent. All in all, it had been a disappointing, unproductive hour.

Somehow, Dani would convince the witness to testify. She believed in the law. More, she believed in justice, even when that justice was overburdened and at times appeared to be as blind as she was often portrayed.

Tension edged along her skin. There was nothing in the upper-class neighborhood, composed of lofts and boutiques and bistros, to produce such a reaction, but the sense of unease that she had been carrying around all day deepened.

On the way back to her car, she stopped. She was being followed. Two blocks earlier, she had sensed it. Now she was certain. Casually she turned, feigned an interest in a storefront window.

A man, tall with dark hair and dark eyes, had made no attempt to conceal his presence. In fact, he kept walking in her direction. There was no ducking into a doorway or pretending to read a magazine and, for a moment, she doubted herself.

But her instincts told her that he was not an ordinary man strolling down the street. He had an alertness to him, a manner of moving like one of the large cats she'd seen at the zoo. Could he be the stalker? Didn't stalkers try to conceal their activities?

She was done being a victim. Before she could talk herself out of it, she spun around and got in his face. "Why are you following me?" Her voice sounded tremulous to her own ears, infuriating her. With a wordless prayer, she held her ground.

With his legs braced wide, arms crossed over his chest and hands tucked into his armpits, the man rolled impressive shoulders. A black T-shirt stretched across a wide chest. Black denim encased long legs.

Her immediate impression was one of power, determination and control. The gaze that met hers was so implacable, so filled with determined purpose that she couldn't look away. There was no hint of mercy in the chilling dark eyes that raked over her, no softening of the mouth that formed a hard line in an equally hard face.

Her throat felt dry. This kind of thirst, though, would not be quenched by mere water; the thirst, the racing pulse, the sweating hands—they were all part of the body's response to imminent threat.

All of her senses felt on fire as adrenaline poured through her bloodstream. Conversely, a chill clambered up her spine. Then, without warning, the fear pouring through her morphed into a different emotion: anger, white-hot and razor sharp.

Her heartbeat thundered, sending blood to her limbs, her muscles; the aching pressure in her chest expanded. Her throat snapped shut. She hadn't had an asthma attack in months, but the shortness of breath was unmistakable.

"I wondered how long it would take for you to catch on." There was no apology in his voice, no attempt to placate her or convince her that she was mistaken. She felt his arm slip around her waist, his firm grasp clearly communicating that this was not the time for her to resist.

That wasn't what she'd expected. In fact, nothing about the man with the hard eyes and unsmiling mouth was what she'd expected, but then, what did she know about stalkers?

"You didn't answer my question," she said and wished her voice didn't sound as if it was about to crack.

"It's my job."

Again, not what she'd expected. "It's your job to follow me?"

"Yes." With more gentleness than she'd credited him with, he steered her to an outdoor café. He seated her at a wrought-iron table, then took the chair opposite her, turned it around and straddled it. He stuck out his hand. "Rabb."

Just that one name, spoken with crisp efficiency. A man who got right down to business. Was that some kind of stalker etiquette?

Dani had the sensation of having fallen down a rabbit's hole and automatically put her hand in his. "Danielle Barclay."

"I know."

"Why are you following me?" She'd get an answer or she was calling the police.

"Your father hired me."

Jake Rabb hadn't wanted this job. Playing bodyguard to one of society's darlings wasn't his style. He'd spent enough time while in the military assigned to consulates where his duties included tending ambassadors' daughters and wives. They had treated him like some kind of lackey who was there to fetch and carry out orders for them.

But a job was a job.

When Shelley, his sister and business partner, had accepted the job from Senator Barclay to protect his only daughter, Jake had balked at being the one to babysit the deputy district attorney.

"You took the job. You play bodyguard," he'd told her.

"I'm already booked."

Jake couldn't argue with that. Shelley had taken the assignment of providing security for the CEO of a plastics firm who had been receiving threats from a far-left environmental group.

S & J Security was barely six months old. The business couldn't afford to turn away any job, especially a high-profile one like this from a United States senator. Given that it was a congressman who had leaked the information about his last mission, a mission that had cost the lives of seven brave men, Jake had no liking for politicians.

"I'm not a babysitter," he'd said. "Get someone else."

"We can't afford to hire anyone else. Besides, the senator asked for you. Seems he was impressed by what he read about you when you left Delta."

The memory caused Jake's lips to twist. Leaving Delta had brought him here, to acting as a bodyguard for a spoiled princess playing at being a deputy district attorney. He'd take fighting an enemy anytime to babysitting.

"How do I know you are who you say you are?" The tart question drew him back to the present.

He looked at his newest client, green eyes glinting, dark red hair aflame, outrage written across her features, and felt a reluctant admiration. He had to outweigh her by eighty or more pounds. It had taken guts to confront him as she had. "Call your father. Ask him."

She pulled her phone from her purse, punched in a number, waited. "Give me a description." She listened, studied Jake, nodded. "Okay. That matches." Her voice grew stronger with every word. "You hired some…thug…to follow me." There was a huskiness in her voice that suggested she was now more angry than frightened.

Atta girl. Anger, he could deal with. Despite the seriousness of the conversation, Jake's lips tipped upward. He'd been called many things over the years, but *thug* was a new one.

"I. Do. Not. Need. A. Bodyguard."

Now they were getting to it. He'd been told the lady was independent to a fault and would likely raise a ruckus at having a bodyguard.

A loud voice from the other end of the line snagged his attention. "Rabb stays."

The two concise words must have ended the conversation, for she stuffed her phone back into her purse. "The senator has spoken."

"Sorry I scared you."

"That was your job, wasn't it? To frighten me into going along with having a bodyguard?" She had him there.

"Sorry, lady, but you didn't hire me. The senator did." He reined in his impatience. "You really think you're dealing with some run-of-the-mill stalker? I heard about the fish. That takes it up a notch."

"How did you know—" She cut her words off. "I should have known. Nobody holds out against the senator."

Jake nodded. "Your father pulled some strings in the police department. Apparently he has someone feeding him information when it comes to anything about you. He knew about this morning's package within an hour of you reporting it."

Her sigh was part frustration, part resignation. "He loves

me. But he can't accept that I don't need his protection. He wants me to move home."

"It's not a bad idea. He's bound to have better security than that apartment building you live in."

"I'm not running home to Daddy just because I have a problem."

"Then you'll stay with my sister and me. You need round-the-clock protection. Our security is so tight that a mouse couldn't get in without us knowing about it."

Dani lifted her chin and looked him directly in the eye. She didn't flinch at the hard-eyed stare he gave in return but held his gaze with boldness and shining courage. "Let's get one thing straight—I'll put up with you following me around, but only for my father's sake. He isn't well, and I won't cause him another moment of distress." Her voice hitched a little. "He had a heart attack last year. He doesn't need any more stress."

Jake understood family obligation, but he heard genuine love for her father in her voice and felt an unexpected moment of accord with her. Although she was angry with her parent, she'd accepted Jake as a bodyguard to soothe her father.

That feeling of accord evaporated with her next words.

"Do you know what it was like while I was growing up? I didn't go to school like the other kids. I was driven by a chauffeur. I had two bodyguards hulking in the shadows." In a gesture similar to his own, she pushed a hand through her hair. "I was never invited to birthday parties. Or anywhere else. I never had a second date, because the boys who asked me out couldn't face being followed everywhere we went." She drew herself up. "I don't like being followed. Or manipulated. Or being treated like some fragile little girl who can't take care of herself."

"Poor little rich girl." He didn't bother masking the contempt in his voice. He wondered what she'd think of the way he'd grown up, fighting his way out of the slums with nothing but his fists and a fierce determination to make a better life for himself and Shelley.

Her head jerked up. At the same time, her expression went smooth as glass. He could see her rebuild a mask of composure, layer by painstaking layer. "Think what you want."

The words were said with a studied lack of concern, but he heard the pain behind them. He had no desire to hurt her, but he wasn't willing to back down from doing his job.

"I have a job to do," he said, as though to reinforce his thoughts…and his resolve. "It'll be a lot easier if you cooperate. But I'm here to stay." To prove his point, Jake cupped her elbow and steered her to his Jeep.

"Have it your way."

"I usually do."

TWO

The D.A.'s offices resembled a rabbit warren, with people scurrying down one corridor, up another.

"We might as well get this over with," Dani said.

Jake heard the resignation in her voice.

It turned out they didn't need to explain Jake's presence. "Your father called," her boss, Leonard Freeman, the district attorney, told her. "He said he'd hired a bodyguard for you."

Dani sighed. "Of course he did." She made the introductions.

Jake stored away impressions. There was the D.A. himself, overweight and jowly, who, despite his self-important manner, seemed genuinely concerned about Dani's safety. Then there were two A.D.A.s, Sarah Whitmore and Trevor Ryan, in the section and, finally, a secretary, Clariss Trenton.

There was little warmth or concern in the gazes they turned on Dani. Instead, there was only a hard-edged gleam of curiosity.

"That everybody?" Jake asked.

"There're two dozen other prosecutors, but you met the ones I work with on a daily basis."

"People, listen up," Freeman said in his foghorn voice. "Dani needs our support, and we'll give it to her. One hundred percent. We're a team here. There is no *I* in team."

"But there is a *me*," Ryan muttered under his breath.

Obviously, he hadn't meant to be overheard and flushed

when Jake raised a brow, letting Ryan know his words hadn't gone unnoticed.

As the day wore on, Jake took stock of Dani's colleagues whom he'd met earlier. Sarah Whitmore and Trevor Ryan seemed friendly enough, even if that friendliness came off as a little forced. They both took the opportunity to express their concern over what Dani was going through.

"If you need anything, anything at all," Whitmore stressed to Dani, "just let me know. I can take over some of your workload if you're not up to it."

Translation: *I can't wait to show the boss what I can do.* The butter-won't-melt voice was so sweet as to be dripping with syrup.

Ryan made the same offer. "You know we're here for you, Dani. Anytime. Any day."

Dani smiled. "Thanks. Both of you. I know you've got my back."

Jake had done his homework before taking on the job. From what he'd learned, Ryan had been passed over for the next-to-top spot that Dani now occupied and wasn't happy about it. He couldn't help wondering if Ryan might want to put a knife in her back, instead of guarding it. And then there was Whitmore, who came off cloying rather than supportive.

If the office reflected the woman, then Dani Barclay was as no-nonsense and straightforward as the plain metal desk that occupied the center of the room. A tired sofa and two equally tired chairs provided dubious seating.

Somehow Jake knew that the less-than-inspired furniture didn't define her, though, especially when he took in the bold impressionistic painting that dominated the room. Slashes of colors should have jarred but didn't, inviting the viewer to take a second…and a third look. Only one other item hinted at anything personal, a small plaque propped on her desk.

Intrigued by the message, he murmured the words aloud. "'Grace happens anyway; the least we can do is be there.'"

Freeman made a point of checking on Dani several times during the afternoon.

"I'd say to take a couple of weeks off, go somewhere this creep can't find you, but the truth is I can't afford to let you go right now." He gestured around, as if to encompass the entire office. "We're understaffed as it is, and you're the best I have."

"Thanks, boss," Dani said and gave him the same little speech she'd given her two coworkers. "He's a good guy," she said to Jake when Freeman took his leave. "A bit self-involved. But he's dedicated to the job. I'm lucky to work for him. I've learned a lot. And he has one of the highest rates of closing cases in the state."

Jake nodded but reserved making a judgment about the D.A. The man was accustomed to being in the spotlight and didn't like sharing it. Dani's troubles had put her on the front page, earning her a notoriety Jake knew she didn't want.

It had been too much to hope that the stalker's antics wouldn't make the news, given that many reporters had connections in the Atlanta Police Department. One reporter in particular, Taryn Starks, had kept the story about Dani's stalker in the papers, dredging up any bit of information to keep it alive. It didn't help matters that Dani was young and attractive, making her an appealing victim. An enterprising photographer had scouted up a picture of her attending a society event.

With Dani busy at her desk, Jake did reconnaissance work. He started with Sarah Whitmore. He found her in the break room, pouring herself a cup of coffee.

"Let me," he said and took the carafe from her.

"Thank you." Her mouth twisted in an expression of concern. "It's awful what's happening to Dani. Just awful."

"I'm sure Dani appreciates your support."

"Anything I can do. Though…" Her voice trailed off suggestively.

"Is there something you know that would help?" he prompted.

"It's only that Dani's a bit of a drama queen. When her mother disappeared, she carried on something terrible. Not that it wasn't perfectly dreadful, of course, but still."

"And you think that has something to do with the stalking?"

She made a point of lowering her voice. "It's only that Dani likes to be the center of attention. Is it possible she's doing this to herself?" She clapped a hand over her mouth. "Forget I said that. Please. It can't be true." But her expression made it plain that she didn't want him to forget it.

Jake filed that away, along with other impressions.

Trevor Ryan was next on his list. With his orthodontically straight teeth and salon-styled hair, the lawyer was handsome enough. Jake supposed he appealed to the ladies, at least on a superficial basis.

"What can I do for you, Rabb?" Ryan asked.

"I'm just trying to get a feel for Dani's day-to-day life. Anything you can tell me would be helpful."

Ryan leaned a hip on his desk and gestured for Jake to take a seat. It wasn't lost on Jake that the other man had intentionally chosen position that put Jake at a disadvantage. Some people were into power games. Something else to be filed away.

"Dani's a good enough lawyer. She carries her own weight—that is, when she's not preoccupied with personal matters."

"And has she been? Preoccupied with personal matters, I mean."

"There's no denying that this stalking thing has taken up her time. Filing reports, meeting with the police, that kind of thing." He shrugged, as if to say it wasn't any of his business.

Jake remained silent, waited for what he knew would come next.

"She does her best, but it's been hard on the rest of us. You could say we've had to carry her. Not that we mind," Ryan added hastily. "Not at all."

"Of course not. Do you have any idea who could be doing this to her?"

"No! I mean, why would I?" Ryan's tone turned hostile.

"Just covering the bases." Jake rose. "Thanks for your time."

"Anything I can do to help. Anything at all."

It didn't take much to read between the lines. Both Whitmore and Ryan were jealous of Dani. Office politics were one thing, but both coworkers seemed determined to cast her in a bad light. Could be nothing. Then again, people had been known to threaten, even kill, for a job.

Suspicion, along with a healthy dose of paranoia, was part of the job. Sometimes it was a big part, other times, not so much. As discomfiting as it was, he'd be a fool to ignore it. And Jake Rabb was no fool.

He'd learned that the only way to deal with it was to make sure it didn't paralyze him.

By the end of the day, Dani was dragging. Her life had taken a one-eighty, and she felt as if it was spinning out of control. Jake Rabb was an unexpected and unwanted complication.

She had initially resisted Jake's directive that she stay with him and his sister and balked at his insistence that she needed 24/7 protection. After some argument, she'd conceded. The memory of her father's sorrow after her mother had gone missing made Dani realize that if something happened to her, he'd be totally devastated and might never recover from it.

A strategic move to a different location wasn't the same as running home to her father and letting him lock her away in an ivory tower. It was a small point, but an important one.

Over Jake's objections, Dani insisted upon returning to her apartment. "If I'm going to stay with you and your sister, I need clothes."

"We get in, and we get out," he said. "Every minute you're there, you're at risk."

His words sounded too much like orders, she thought with annoyance. He was instinctively trying to take control. That was just what she had been wary of, turning her life over to someone else.

He pulled out his phone. "I need to call my sister, let her know we'll be running late."

The short conversation revealed little about the man, except when he ended with "death to our enemies."

When he hung up, Dani slanted a curious look his way. "What was that?"

"A code Shelley and I devised a while back."

"You need a code to talk with your sister?"

"A safety measure we set up."

At the lobby to her building, Dani stopped.

"Hi, Ms. Barclay." The familiar voice of the doorman had her lips lifting in her first real smile of the day. At twenty-two, Barry Thomas was nearly ten years younger than herself. Even so, he was married with a baby on the way.

She knew he and his wife struggled to make ends meet and made it a point to tip him well.

"Thank you, ma'am," he said and folded the bill she slipped him inside his pocket.

His fresh-faced looks and use of the word *ma'am* made her feel impossibly old. She shook her head at her musings. She was hardly over the hill, but sometimes she felt the years slipping by and at odd moments found herself wishing for someone to share her life with. Resolutely, she pushed that away and gave Barry her attention.

"How's Suzanne feeling?"

He grimaced. "Tired all the time. Says her feet hurt. But she wants to keep working until the baby comes." His young face flushed. "I told her to stay home and rest, but we need the money."

Dani made sympathetic noises and made a mental note to send a gift when the baby arrived.

"Oh, I almost forgot. There's a package for you," Barry said and started to hand the gaily wrapped gift to her.

Up until then, Jake had stayed in the background. Now he moved in front of her to intercept the package. "Who delivered this? When? Did you have to sign for it?"

Barry looked confused and more than a little alarmed at the barrage of questions Jake fired at him. "Ms. Barclay?"

Jake jerked the man's attention back to him. "I'm the one asking the questions."

"It's all right, Barry," Dani said gently. "Just answer the questions the best you can."

"A messenger showed up about forty-five minutes ago. He gave me the package, asked that I hand deliver it to you."

"That's fine," Dani said. "Thank you." Once they were out of earshot, she rebuked Jake. "You scared him." Jake had scared her as well, but she wouldn't give voice to the words.

"We've got to make a detour. We're taking this to the Atlanta P.D."

The police department was a cacophony of voices, the scrape of chairs against the hard linoleum floor and the clatter of keyboards, underlaid with the scent of bad coffee and industrial cleanser. It differed only a little from army barracks, and Jake felt immediately at home.

Dani in her light pink suit and heels earned a few whistles and admiring turns of heads, but she strode through the squad room with a familiarity that impressed Jake and knocked at a door.

Purposeful. That was the way Dani walked, like a woman who knew what needed to be done and got on with it.

She made the introductions with a minimum of words. "Detective Monroe." She jerked a thumb in Jake's direction. "Jake Rabb. I've acquired a bodyguard," she said to Monroe. "My father's idea."

The two men sized each other up. Jake decided he liked what he saw. With skin the color of a walnut and a beard more gray than black, Monroe had the look of a man who had seen the worst the world had to offer and decided to see what he could do about it.

Monroe nodded in acknowledgment. "It's a good one. We don't have the manpower to guard you day and night."

"I never asked for that."

"No. That's why he—" the detective gestured at Jake "—is a good idea. Let's take a look at what we've got here." Donning latex gloves, Monroe opened the package. A dead bird lay nestled in a bed of straw.

Jake had to hand it to Dani. She didn't gasp or cry out, viewed the contents of the box with stoic calm. Only the tightening of her lips had given any hint as to her feelings.

Detective Monroe took the box, promised he'd have the lab examine it, but didn't hold out much hope in finding anything. "Whoever's been doing this has been too careful to leave any prints or anything else we can trace."

"There's always a chance he's slipped up," Dani said.

"There's a chance." But the dismal tone in his voice belied his words.

In the meantime, Jake couldn't help noticing the easy camaraderie she enjoyed with Monroe, as well as the other men and women who worked there. Despite the strain she was obviously under, she'd made a point of asking about families, smiling when a grizzled officer had shown her pictures of his newest grandchild.

It was apparent that they regarded Dani as one of their own. It was also apparent that they were fiercely protective of her.

"I'm glad you're on the case," Detective Monroe confided to Jake in a private moment. "We're doing our best, but we're spread too thin." He made a disgusted sound. "Budget cuts. As if it weren't hard enough to do our jobs, the city fathers decide we need to 'trim the fat.' Look around you. You see any fat?" His lips flattened as he gestured to the sparsely furnished squad room with its utilitarian office equipment.

Jake empathized with the older man's frustration. He'd seen the effects that budget cuts had on the army. Substandard or outdated equipment had cost more than one botched operation.

He cast a glance in Dani's direction. "What's your honest opinion of what's going on?"

Monroe rubbed his chin. "Prosecutors make enemies. No getting around it. Dani handles her share of cases, some of them nasty as all get-out. But, for the most part, the people she prosecutes aren't stupid. They're mean, cunning and greedy, but they know that if she's taken off a case, someone else will be assigned. Scaring her off isn't going to change anything. Not in the long run."

Jake had nodded. The detective's assessment matched his own. Not that he wouldn't check out the cases she was handling, but these threats didn't feel as if they were coming from an outsider. They felt personal.

That, in his opinion, made them all the more dangerous.

"What do we do?" Dani asked as she and Jake left the police department, and the first hint of fear slipped into her voice.

Silently he applauded her attitude. She didn't bury her head in the sand, pretending she wasn't under attack. No, she wanted to know what they were going to do.

At least she was including him.

"I don't know." She deserved honesty from him. At the same time, she needed reassurance. "But I can promise you one thing—whoever is doing this is going to have to go through me to get to you."

"Thank you."

"For what?"

"For being honest." And then, a heartbeat later, "And for being here."

That cost her, he thought.

"That bird, to break its neck that way." She made an impatient gesture, the derision clearly directed at herself. "I know. I deal with murderers, rapists, the worst society can offer, every day. But this…" She shook her head. "I had a canary when I was a little girl. Somehow it got out of its cage one day. It flew into a plate-glass window, broke its neck on impact. Funny. I hadn't thought of that in years. This brought it back."

Jake's interest sharpened. "Who knows that story?"

She looked startled. "A few people, I guess. My parents. A couple of friends at the office. Anyone who worked for my family during that time. Why? The bird in the package…that's just a coincidence. A horrible coincidence." She paused. "Isn't it?"

Jake didn't believe in coincidences. Not when it came to protecting a client. In his experience, coincidences masked convenient opportunities.

At her apartment, Jake had Dani wait outside the door while he went through the place. Gun drawn, he checked every room, including closets and underneath the bed.

When he determined that all was clear, he gave her the

go-ahead. "Bring enough for a week," he said. "We don't know how long you'll be gone."

For a second, her shoulders drooped. Then she straightened, stared him in the eye and said, "Let's get this creep. I want my life back."

Once again, Jake gave her points for fighting back. The lady was determined not to be a victim.

The trip to Jake's home gave Dani a chance to sort through her impressions about her unwanted bodyguard. She was still fuming over his high-handed attitude.

She set that aside and studied him from beneath her eyelashes. Military. It was obvious now. The ramrod posture, the buzz cut, the way he had of issuing orders and expecting to be obeyed. She'd confirmed her guess by checking him out on the computer and had learned that he'd been part of Delta Force.

He had a quiet alertness to him that was at once reassuring and unnerving, for it reminded her of the purpose for his presence. A powerful man, she mused. In looks. In manner. In basic appeal. But it wasn't power that she sensed now. It was determination.

The whitewashed brick house set in an older neighborhood came as a surprise. She'd expected something ultramodern, not the homey picture it suggested. That picture, though, was belied by the high-tech security that protected the house.

Jake punched in a set of numbers, followed by another set. Before he entered, he told Dani to wait outside while he swept the room with his gun drawn.

At her raised brow, he said, "You don't go anywhere before I check it out first. Even here."

Inside, he introduced her to his sister and filled Shelley in on the latest threat.

Shelley Rabb listened, nodded, made a few notes for herself.

Dani was immediately drawn to the other woman. Shelley had eyes more blue than gray, dark hair cut close to her head and a quirky smile. A few keystrokes on the computer earlier in the afternoon had netted Dani the information that Shelley had once served as a Secret Service agent.

"You don't look like an ex–Secret Service agent," Dani said. "I mean—"

Jake draped an arm around his sister's shoulders. "No, she doesn't. Probably what made her so good at her job."

"And don't you forget it," Shelley said with a mock growl. "I hope you weren't fooled by this one," she said, motioning to Jake.

"I'm beginning to get the picture." Dani enjoyed the by-play between Jake and his sister. They were opposite types physically, but she sensed the deep affection they had for each other. While growing up she had wished she'd had a brother or a sister. Hers had been a lonely childhood in many ways. She pushed away the old regret. She'd been raised in a home filled with love and laughter. She had no cause to complain.

"Has he pulled his macho military stuff on you yet?" Shelley asked.

For the first time in hours, Dani smiled. "You could say that."

"Don't let him get away with it. Underneath all that bluff and bluster, he's a lamb."

That earned a snort from Jake. "Why don't you show Dani to a room?"

Shelley took Dani to a tastefully decorated bedroom, the aqua-and-cream color scheme quietly soothing.

"Make yourself at home."

"Thank you. It's beautiful."

"Dinner in an hour. It's Jake's night to cook."

The dinner of spaghetti with clam sauce, salad and garlic bread was delicious. It was simple but filling, and Dani helped herself to a second serving. "Where did you learn to cook like this?" she asked Jake.

A shadow passed over his face, but it was Shelley who answered. "Jake was cooking for us before he turned nine."

Where were their parents? Dani wondered but kept the question to herself.

"I'll clean up," she volunteered. The prosaic duties of clearing and rinsing dishes and stacking them in the dishwasher helped settle her thoughts after a chaotic day.

"Jake's a great cook," Shelley said upon joining her, "but he can't scramble an egg without dirtying every pan in the kitchen." Her smile curved with a blend of affection and exasperation.

Dani surveyed the kitchen and had to agree.

"If you two have finished gossiping, Dani and I have some talking to do."

She knew what was coming and dreaded it. The last thing she wanted to do was dissect her past. "I've got a brief to write."

"It can wait. I want a list of the names of people who knew about your canary." Before she could react to that, he added, "We're going to have to go over your case list tomorrow."

She squared her shoulders. "I know."

"Plus your coworkers, your friends."

"You can't seriously suspect any of them."

"Until I get this guy, I suspect everyone. And I am going to get him."

She stiffened. He sounded just like her father and Victor, a onetime boyfriend and now friend, telling her what to do, expecting her to obey their orders, while coddling her at the same time. She'd worked too hard for her independence to relinquish it.

Jake's expression remained implacable. With his military background, it was natural for him to give orders, but that didn't mean she had to like them.

"Trust me," he said. "I know what I'm doing."

Trust me. Two small words, but so difficult for her to accept.

"Okay," she said in a resigned voice and struggled to smother a surge of frustration, reminding herself that Jake was only trying to do his job. "Where do I start?"

"Make a list of anyone who knows about your childhood, especially those who knew about the bird. Family. Friends. Attendants who used to work for your family."

"Okay. Then what?"

"Then we find out what those people are doing now. Where they're living. Where they're working. If they're here in Atlanta or have moved away."

"That's a tall order."

"We've got to start somewhere. After we do that, we start ruling out those who don't live in the state."

"How far back do I go?" she asked.

"As far as you can."

Dani started with the present and worked her way backward. The list grew as she recalled the various gardeners, housemaids, grooms, cooks and others who had worked for her family. The list of her friends was a much smaller one. Intimidated by her father's position and the grandeur of the house, few friends had come to visit. Boyfriends had been put off by the bodyguards who were her constant companions.

She had regarded those few boys intrepid enough to tolerate the bodyguards with suspicion. Were they attracted to her or her family's wealth and background? As a result, she had been wary of any man who had shown too much interest. She'd had only one serious relationship, and it had ended four years ago.

Trust didn't come easily, especially after she'd joined the D.A.'s office and seen what men and women could do to one another.

Jake gave a low whistle as he read the list of people who had worked for her family. "Just how big is your parents' home?"

"The house itself is fairly large, the grounds over a hundred acres. They take a lot of work."

"I'm beginning to get the picture."

By midnight, Dani was weary beyond belief and ready to call it quits. Jake, however, seemed to have an inexhaustible supply of energy.

"Enough," she said after he'd questioned her over and over. It was bad enough that someone hated her enough to threaten her. To be grilled about people she considered friends, even family, was too much. "Enough."

She rose and, without another word, went to her bedroom and shut the door behind her.

Jake rose every morning at four-thirty. He headed to the weight room he'd added at the back of the house and pushed himself for the next forty-five minutes, sweating out painful memories that still had the power to cause his gut to contract.

There'd been a time when he could scarcely lift his injured leg off an exercise mat and had resisted the therapy prescribed by his doctor. After a while, he'd used it as a kind of punishment for the fact that he had lived and seven of his men had died during the botched mission in Libya. The pain had been excruciating, but he'd pushed his way through it.

He shoved aside the images and considered his newest client. He hadn't wanted to bring Dani to his home, but it seemed the best way to protect her. Maybe he'd been too quick to paint her as a spoiled princess. Maybe. He was reserving judgment.

She'd held up during the trip to the police department and viewing the dead bird, an experience that would have sent many into hysterics.

When Dani appeared in the weight room a couple of hours later, dressed and obviously ready for work, he gave a start. "You're going to work?"

"I've got seven cases. I can't afford to take a day off."

"I thought—"

"—that I was just playing at being deputy district attorney and take off whenever the whim hits me?" She stopped his protest with a lift of her hand and gave him an unsmiling look. "I get that a lot. Whatever you think of me personally, Rabb, I take my work seriously."

After questioning her about the past last night, she'd been pale, fragile and shivering. That vulnerable woman was gone. Today, there was a resolute firmness about her. She was dressed in a red suit that shouted confidence.

The result was professional, competent and, at the same time, totally feminine.

"Give me ten minutes." He showered and dressed in record time.

They made the drive to the city building in near silence, each caught up in their own thoughts.

At Dani's office, Jake made himself comfortable on a sagging sofa and booted up his laptop. He ought to be able to do a cursory check on the names she'd given him last night. Nothing was private anymore.

Two hours later, he had made considerable inroads into the list of names. Those who had worked for Dani's family were clean, no records, not even a whiff of any illegal activities. More important, from the stalking standpoint, there was no hint that any of them had cause to bear a grudge against Dani.

"I need to know about the people you're prosecuting."

Her brow knit in concentration, she gave him a distracted look. "I can't discuss ongoing cases."

"I think you can make an exception, given the circumstances."

Dani pulled files from her desk, handed them to him. "You can start here."

After another hour of reading, he looked up and studied Dani, who was currently bent over a legal pad. "I didn't think anyone used those anymore."

"I'm old-school."

A knock at the door had them both looking up.

"Ms. Barclay...I mean, Dani, Victor Wingate's on the phone." The secretary darted a nervous look between her boss and Jake. "Shall I take a message?"

"Please."

Clariss backed out of the office.

"Who's Victor Wingate?"

"A defense attorney. He and I have faced off on a few cases over the years."

"Anything else?"

"We dated for several months. Things were serious for a while. Then they weren't."

Jake pulled out the notebook he kept in his pocket and scribbled down the name. "Do you still see him?"

"Once in a while, when one of us has something we have to go to and can't get out of."

"Was it his choice or yours when it stopped being serious?"

"It was mutual."

Jake doubted it. No man would willingly give up a woman like Dani. She had it all. Looks. Intelligence. Class. Then he remembered another woman, also lovely and appealing, also the daughter of a wealthy, powerful man, only to find that she was shallow beneath the pretty exterior. Hadn't he learned his lesson?

Love, or even a relationship, wasn't for him. Especially not now, when he carried around more than his share of baggage.

He pushed that away. This wasn't about him. He checked his watch, saw that it was past noon. "How about lunch?"

"I usually order in."

Another surprise. He'd figured her for eating at one of the trendy restaurants that dotted the city.

"Sorry to disappoint you," she said.

"You didn't."

Over sandwiches, chips and soda, he pumped her. "Tell me about your cases."

Dani put down her sandwich and wiped her mouth. "You read the files."

"I want your impressions. What your gut tells you."

Whether or not it was because she didn't know whom she could trust, Dani opened up about her cases.

She gestured to the fattest file. "Jerry Brooks. He beat his wife until she could barely stand. I finally convinced her to file charges and go to a safe house. He promised he'd kill her if he got his hands on her again. He's currently out on bail.

"He's the worst kind of bully. He thinks he's above the law because he's a city councilman." Her lips quirked. "Or he was. It seems his constituents frown on members beating their wives senseless and sent him packing. He works at a mechanic's shop now."

"So he's been humiliated in front of his peers." A powerful motive for revenge.

"He doesn't scare me."

"Maybe he should." Jake lifted another file. "What about this one? A woman accused of elder abuse."

Dani nodded. "Patricia Newton. She's a home health

aide, wormed her way into an elderly man's life. It seems he felt sorry for her because she came from the Middle East and was having a hard time getting a job. Turns out Newton was forging Mr. McBride's name on credit cards the entire time she was supposed to be caring for him."

"That's rotten, but it doesn't sound like something for your office."

"You're right. It wouldn't be. Ordinarily it would go to another prosecutor. In this case, though, the woman was systematically poisoning her client. It was only because his daughter arrived and found him comatose that he's still alive."

"Nice."

"She's out on bail, too."

"What's with the court, letting scum like those two out on bail?"

Dani massaged her temples with her fingertips. "The court's job is to grant bail if it sees fit. It's my job to make sure Newton and Brooks don't have a chance to hurt anyone else."

"You care." Jake pointed to the files. "You care about the victims. That's why you do this. You could have had your choice of any of the big firms in town, but you went with the D.A.'s office."

"You get it. No one really has. Certainly not my father." The last was said with some irony. "He's devoted his entire life to serving, first on the bench, then in the state legislature, then on the national level. But he doesn't get why I need to do what I do."

"What about your mother?" He'd learned that Madeline Barclay had disappeared four years ago and hadn't been seen since.

"My mother didn't understand either. She tried. She was coming around to accepting what I did when she went missing." Dani cast him a shrewd look. "But you knew that, didn't you?"

"Yeah. I knew."

"My father hired the best agency in the South to find her. They didn't turn up one clue as to where she went. Or why."

Jake moved closer. "I'm sorry. That must hurt." Some pains didn't go away. He ought to know.

After their mother had walked out on him and Shelley, he'd done his best to protect his little sister, to buffer her from the reality that their mother had left them without a second thought. No way did he want her to feel as worthless and unwanted as he had, but she was too smart and had already figured out for herself that their mother hadn't loved them.

As he'd grown older, he wondered if his mother's abandonment had played into his reluctance to fully give his heart to a woman. Something had always held him back but for one momentary lapse. Maybe it was a lack of trust. Or maybe he just didn't have it in him to truly love.

He pushed away the unwanted memories and focused on what Dani was saying.

"It hurts every day," she admitted. "Every day. But I've learned to live with it. Victor was a big help back then. He fielded calls, was there to hold my hand when I was ready to fall apart. We grew close."

"What happened?"

"He started being clingy. Rather, he wanted *me* to be clingy. Things got awkward. We finally parted ways. But we're still friends."

"Why?"

"Why what?"

"Why do you go with him instead of someone else?"

She appeared to think about it. "Convenience, I suppose. We know each other. We don't have to worry about things getting serious."

"And this Victor. He doesn't mind escorting you when he knows nothing's going to come of it?"

"He's okay with it, I guess." But her voice lacked certainty.

"But you're not sure."

"Why are you asking about Victor? He was there for me when my mother disappeared. He's been a good friend."

"I'm trying to get a fix on who's in your life. Whoever's doing this knows you. Knows how to get to you." He didn't bother softening the words. He wouldn't be doing his job if he downplayed the danger.

"You'd do better to concentrate on the people I'm prosecuting. None of my friends or colleagues have any reason to hurt me."

"You'd be surprised by why people feel they have reason to carry a grudge," Jake said. "I've seen one tribe decimate another because of a slight to the chief's daughter."

Dani pointed a finger to herself. "I'm hardly one to be surprised at what one person can do to another. I'm a D.D.A, remember? I've seen it all."

He doubted that. "Then you ought to know better than to take people at face value." He saw that his words weren't going over well.

A knock at the door made her look up. "Come in."

Clariss stood there, a quietly pleading look on her face. "I'm sorry, Dani. I couldn't stop him."

An impatient man brushed past her. "Dani, darling. When I heard what happened, I had to see you."

He started to round the desk, but Jake blocked his way. When the man tried to get past him, Jake refused to budge.

The man turned a hurt gaze in Dani's direction. "What's going on?"

"It's all right, Jake," she said, placing a restraining hand on his arm. "Victor's a friend." She turned to Victor. "Jake's my bodyguard until this mess is over."

Victor Wingate regarded Jake with frank skepticism. "A bodyguard, huh? Is that really necessary? I mean, you've got the police department."

"It wasn't my idea," Dani said. "My father hired him."

Wingate nodded. "I see. I'm pleased that you're taking precautions."

"Are you?" Jake challenged. He took stock of the man. So this was the ex-boyfriend. Blond hair, worn a little long for Jake's taste. South Beach tan. Trendy clothes that screamed, "Look at me." A Breitling watch on his left wrist that cost more than Jake's first car.

Wingate had the bland good looks and cocky self-assurance that, Jake supposed, some women might find attractive, if they were the type to be impressed by two-hundred-dollar haircuts and pricey watches.

Wingate appeared to take umbrage at Jake's question. "What are you implying? Dani is special to me. Of course I'm glad she has protection."

"Then you won't mind buzzing off. Dani's had a hard day and needs to get home."

"Is that what you want, Dani?" the man asked.

"It has been a long day," she confessed. "But I appreciate you stopping by, Victor. Maybe we can catch up later."

"Of course. Just know that I'm here for you. Whatever you need." He bent to kiss her, narrowing his eyes when she turned her cheek toward him rather than her lips.

Jake barely kept from snorting. Wingate's pretty-boy looks and superior manner set his teeth on edge. He'd run up against a few such officers in the army, full of themselves and more interested in strutting their power than serving their country.

"You were rough on him," Dani said after Wingate saw himself out.

"I'm here to protect you, not make nice with your boyfriend."

"Ex-boyfriend. Victor's no threat. His biggest sin is defending the creeps of the world." She swiped a hand across her brow. "Sorry. I try not to judge the people I prosecute, but sometimes… You were right. It has been a hard day."

Jake grabbed her jacket and her purse, handed both to her. "C'mon. Let's get you home."

"I won't say no."

Jake took a different route to his house than they'd used yesterday. At her raised brow, he explained, "Never take the same route home twice in a row. Routine makes it easier to be followed."

His words made sense. And she wished they didn't.

"How does pizza sound when we get home?" he asked.

"Sounds great. But what about Shelley?"

"She texted me. She won't be home for a few hours."

While Jake ordered a large pizza with the works, Dani changed into jeans and a sweatshirt.

After hanging up her suit, she knelt by her bed. "Dear Lord, thank You for Your constant care. Thank You for keeping me safe. And thank You for sending Jake. I know I didn't want him here, but I need him."

She closed the prayer, but remained on her knees. For most of the day, she had to answer to others. This time was for herself and for listening to the Lord's voice. She knew He was there, guiding her.

After a long moment, she stood and rejoined Jake in the living room.

"Pizza'll be here in twenty minutes," he said.

"Good. I'm starving."

When the pizza arrived, they made short work of it, arguing over who got the last piece.

In the end, they split it.

"I love pizza," Dani said, dabbing at her mouth with a napkin.

"No kidding. I was lucky to get a piece."

"Is that a case of the pot calling the kettle black?"

"No. It's me telling you that you eat like a truck driver." He held up a hand. "Don't apologize."

"I wasn't going to." She flashed a smile. "My mother was always telling me to eat like a lady, to take tiny, little bites and to never let anyone see that I was enjoying the food."

"Sounds pretty foolish."

"Mother was a true lady and was frequently appalled at my behavior." Her smile faded. "It didn't keep me from loving her, though. Or her from loving me."

"You miss her."

"Every day."

"Do you have any idea what happened to her?" A frown pulled his dark eyebrows together, as though he was trying to make sense of something that would never jell. Hadn't she wondered the same? Her mother's disappearance had never added up.

"As I told you, my father hired the best investigators there were. They couldn't find anything. At last, we had to accept that she didn't want to be found." Dani was sorry to hear the note of bitterness that clogged her throat with those last words. Hadn't she promised herself that she was finished grieving?

She'd discovered, though, that grief had no timetable.

"Was she troubled about something before she disappeared? Worried? Did she have a problem with anyone?"

Dani shook her head. "Everyone loved Mother. My father most of all. He adored her. She was the only one who could stand up to him and get him to back down."

"I'd say you do pretty well in that department yourself."

Grateful to remember good times, she smiled. "I'm not in Mother's league. She could have him eating out of her hand with only a flutter of her lashes."

Things had taken a big shift over the past day and a half,

she reflected. Far from resenting Jake's presence in her life, she was beginning to depend on him, and not just for protection. He had a way of keeping her on an even keel. For that alone, she had reason to be grateful to him.

After a moment's reflection, she felt herself pulling back from her thoughts. She'd been grateful to a man before, and it had turned out badly. Gratitude alone wasn't enough on which to base a relationship. She'd learned that lesson the hard way and wasn't about to forget it.

She realized she'd been talking about herself without attempting to get to know him better and asked, "Are you and your mother close?"

Jake's eyes went cold. "I haven't seen my mother in over twenty years. She abandoned Shelley and me as soon as I could get a job."

"I'm sorry." She winced at the inadequacy of the words.

"It doesn't matter."

But it did. Judging from his expression, it mattered very much. Dani still grieved over her mother's disappearance, her heart twisting in remembered pain, but at least they'd had a loving relationship for many years.

Jake had been denied that. Her heart went out to him, but she knew better than to offer any further words of sympathy. When she gazed at him, she saw that his eyes were shadowed with his own memories and with empathy for hers.

"Don't waste your sympathy on me," he said, echoing her thoughts. "Shell and I got along fine. It's been the two of us for as long as I can remember. I made sure she always knew she was loved. I always will."

Dani nodded. "I'm sure you took good care of your sister." She wanted to say more, but what was there to say? She couldn't insist that his mother had cared about him and his sibling when she obviously hadn't. Her heart ached for the young boy and his little sister.

"What about your father?"

"Our old man was never around. He took off before Shelley was born. He said he couldn't stand one brat, much less two. When I was fifteen, our mother left. I guess she figured I was old enough to take care of Shelley. Truth was, she was never much of a mother even when she was there.

"I made up my mind then and there that Shelley would always know that she was loved unconditionally—by me."

Dani pictured a lanky teenage boy trying to hold down a job, go to school and take care of a little sister.

"Shelley is the best thing in my life. She started the business. She probably saved my life when she asked me to join her. I was on the fast track to nowhere."

The quiet intensity in his voice reached down inside Dani, and she felt her heart constrict. Jake was more than she'd first thought. Much more.

THREE

They started with Jerry Brooks. A man who put his wife in the hospital, then threatened her life wouldn't be above sending the prosecuting attorney hate mail and nasty gifts.

Jake and Dani found Brooks at his job at a garage.

The smells of diesel and cigarette smoke combined in a rancid brew that caused her throat to tickle and her eyes to water.

Dani spoke first. "Hello, Mr. Brooks."

A beefy man with hands the size of a small engine block looked up, swiped a grimy hand over his face. "You." He divided a glare between Jake and Dani. "Who's he?"

"The name's Rabb," Jake answered. "Jake Rabb. We're looking into some threats made on Ms. Barclay."

Brooks made a rude noise. "Whoever's doing it, more power to him."

The look he sent in Dani's direction was so filled with venom that Jake was surprised she didn't flinch, but she held her ground.

"You cost me my marriage, my job, my position in the community. I had a good life. You took that from me. You took everything." Brooks gestured around him. "Look at me. I'm a grease monkey." He pulled up his pant leg. "I have to wear this thing day in and day out."

Jake saw the ankle monitor. "From where I'm standing, you're the one who's cost yourself everything."

Brooks slammed a wrench against a workbench, then

advanced toward Dani, his expression one of pure hatred. In one quick movement, Jake put himself between Brooks and Dani. "You stuck your nose in where it doesn't belong." Spittle collected at the corners of his mouth, flecked his face. "A man's got a right to give his wife a cuff when she needs it. The Bible gives him that right." Self-righteousness hung in every word.

"Check again," Dani said. "Nowhere does it say a man's got the right to beat his wife senseless."

Jake kept his hands at his sides with an effort. "No man worthy of the name hits a woman."

"Keep your stinking advice to yourself," Brooks said, big fists raised.

Jake almost wished the man would take a swing at him. Let him see what it felt like to face an opponent who could fight back. "Tell us where you were two nights ago."

Brooks pointed to the monitor. "You want to know where I was, check with the records on this thing." Bitterness rang in every syllable.

"We will."

"You ask me," he said with a sneer in Dani's direction, "you got what's coming to you. Give you a taste of your own medicine."

"You'll have your day in court, Mr. Brooks. Until then, stay away from me and your wife." She turned on her heel.

"He's a piece of work," Jake said as he and Dani walked out of the dark garage into the sunlight.

"He is that. He seems to think that I'm the cause of all his problems."

"A man like that will never admit he's in the wrong, that his problems are of his own making. He'll always have an excuse of why it's not his fault."

Once more, Dani was struck by how Jake cut to the heart of the matter. He was right about Brooks. The man was so caught up in his own arrogance that he would always put his faults onto someone else.

Their next stop was to see Patricia Newton. Her third-floor walk-up was in a run-down building where the stairway was filled with the smells of cooking cabbage and onions, and of garbage that had sat too long. Shouts, a baby's cry and the blare of a television competed for attention. Jake took Dani's hand as they stepped over shards of broken glass.

He rapped on the door.

A blowsy-looking brunette opened it. "What do you want?"

Jake pushed past her and, without waiting to be asked, took a seat. "To talk."

Newton sent Dani a look of pure loathing. "What's she doing here?"

"Good to see you, too," Dani said with heavy irony and sat opposite Jake. Her smile was tiger bright as she regarded the other woman.

"Someone's been making threats against Ms. Barclay," Jake said. "After you were found guilty, you promised you'd get even with her."

Newton lowered her considerable bulk into an easy chair, its seams barely contained with layers of duct tape. She leaned forward, looking comfortable despite her obvious displeasure at her visitors' appearance. "Yeah, so what?"

Home advantage, Jake thought. She was the one with the favor to grant. He and Dani were merely supplicants. He didn't care for the feeling. "She's been receiving threatening letters and phone calls."

"Wish I'd thought of it." Bitterness dripped from Newton's voice. And something more. Satisfaction. "She said I tried to kill that old man, when all I did was take care of him. If it weren't for me, he'd have croaked months ago."

"If you call poisoning him taking care of him." Jake

didn't bother trying to keep the contempt from his voice. Anyone who conned a senior citizen deserved what she got.

Newton jerked a thumb in Dani's direction. "That's what she says."

That didn't deserve a response, and Jake didn't bother giving one. He posed the same question he'd asked Brooks. "Where were you two nights ago?"

"None of your business."

"I'm making it my business. Tell me, or we can have a chat with the nice detective at the Atlanta P.D."

"I was at home."

"Any witnesses?"

"No. I did not think to need an alibi."

"A word of advice—find someone to back up your story. The police will be paying you a call."

"You have no right to accuse me. I am innocent. Maybe the judge…he will go easy on me." A pious expression crossed Newton's face, and her voice suddenly developed a decided and convenient accent. "I am foreigner here. I do not know all the laws."

Jake seriously doubted that. The woman was a scam artist. She looked out for herself and nobody else. "Try it on someone who'll believe you."

All pretense of piety and innocence had vanished. Her face hardened as she glared at Dani. "I hope you get what you deserve."

It was with relief that Jake and Dani took their leave.

Though he believed in treating everyone, regardless of their standing, with respect, Jake had no use for Patricia Newton. Anyone who took advantage of an elderly man didn't deserve his—or anyone else's—respect. He sincerely hoped the woman received the maximum sentence for her crimes.

Still, neither Newton nor Brooks gave off any vibe of having sent the threatening letters or the gruesome gifts.

Dani was right. They were both bullies, preying on those who were weaker and vulnerable, but they lacked the patience, the planning to execute the terrifying tactics with which she was dealing.

He'd check both Brooks and Newton out further. He couldn't afford to overlook anything or anyone, but he had a feeling Dani's stalker was closer to home.

That filled him with a dread he couldn't shake. Despite her job, Dani was too trusting. She believed herself to be tough and invincible, when the truth was she had a vulnerability about her that called to him on a level he didn't want to acknowledge.

And that, more than anything else, scared him.

Remaining heart-whole had never been a problem, except for a brief lapse with a woman who had been only using him. He'd quickly gotten over any feelings for the woman.

He wouldn't allow himself to be vulnerable to a woman again. His mother had taught him well.

"What did you think of Brooks and Newton?" Dani asked once she and Jake were back at her office. She was anxious for his impressions of the two. Jake had a sharp mind, a way of looking at things that brought them into focus.

She honestly didn't think the two had anything to do with her stalking, but she wanted to know what he thought.

"You were right about them. Bullies. Ready to prey upon anyone they perceive as weaker than themselves. But I don't think they're who we're looking for. They don't have the imagination for it."

"That's what I thought. They don't have the patience for this kind of thing. They're motivated by instant gratification. Power. Money."

Jake nodded. "Another thing—if Brooks were behind this, he'd arrange it so that he could see your fear. He feeds on that. He'd want to see your reaction, your revulsion, your terror."

"And Newton?"

"Newton's motivated by greed. Unless there's something in it for her, she can't be bothered. It's no wonder she chose poison as her weapon. She's filled with venom."

She'd been right about Jake's perception. "You're good at reading people."

He dipped his head. "I have my moments."

That got a laugh from her. "Yes, you do." The laughter died from her eyes. "We're back where we started, aren't we?" Discouragement dragged at her. She wanted this over. She wanted her life back.

"No. We're ruling out who isn't behind this. The more people we rule out, the closer we come to finding out who is."

"Thanks. I needed to hear that." A chill peppered her arms, and she rubbed her hands over them. "I'm scared, Jake."

It cost her to say that. Admitting fear didn't come easily. She'd fought too long and too hard to get where she was to give in to it, but that didn't change the fact that she was spooked, especially after the delivery of the dead bird.

Her willingness to share such feelings with Jake surprised her. Then again, maybe it shouldn't, since she didn't know whom she could trust.

Jake was right. Someone she knew was doing this.

The idea that a colleague or friend, someone close to her, was trying to terrify her filled her with revulsion as well as bafflement. What had she done to inspire such hatred? She knew Trevor and Sarah were jealous of her position, but she didn't regard them as enemies. Try as she would, she couldn't think of anyone she'd hurt so badly as to do this. She was a loner in many ways, keeping to herself. Her circle of friends was a small one, but she'd believed they were devoted to each other.

"Why?" The single word came out in a broken cry. "Why is someone doing this to me?"

Jake drew her to him, cradled her head against his chest. "I don't know. But I promise you—we're going to find out."

She clung to him, drawing comfort from his words as well as the solid feel of him. It wasn't like her to cling to a man. Nothing about this was like her at all.

After a long moment, Jake set her away from him. "We've got work to do."

She scrubbed her hands over her face as though scrubbing away her earlier fear. "Let's get to it."

"One more thing—I want to have a code word between us. If someone gives you a message, supposedly from me, make sure they give you that word." At the question in her eyes, he said, "Just an added security measure."

Dani didn't have to think about it. "Grace."

"Grace? Why that?"

"Everything I have, everything I am, is because of God's grace." So intent was she on their conversation that she scarcely registered the sound of her office door closing.

On Sunday, Dani got ready for church, choosing a peach-colored dress and matching jacket.

"Nothing's going to happen to me at church," she said when Jake protested her decision.

"Our guy's not the boogeyman who's going to jump out at you from a dark alley," Jake said. "He's someone who you know, someone who knows you. And," he added significantly, "he knows your schedule. He knows where and when you attend church."

In the end, Dani won. She wasn't going to let whoever was doing this take away her Sunday worship.

The service was beautiful in its simplicity, and Dani basked in the quiet words of instruction and prayer.

Following its conclusion, the minister, a family friend, looked at Dani with concern. "You look lovely as always, Dani, but tired. Is something wrong?"

Unwilling to burden him with her problems, she shook her head. "I guess I am tired. Too many cases."

The minister nodded. "Your father tells me how hard you work." He winked. "We see each other on the golf course every once in a while. I wish he would join you at services on Sundays."

Dani swallowed. "Ever since my mother…ever since she left, Dad's been distant. He has this block about church, religion. I know he still believes, but…" She lifted a shoulder in a small shrug. "It's been hard." Her mother's disappearance had affected Dani and her father differently. He'd turned away from his faith while Dani clung to hers, as the only constant in a mixed-up world.

She didn't trust herself to say anything more. First, she had to let the lump that was crowding her throat dissolve, otherwise she knew the silent tears that were building behind her eyes would trickle down her cheeks.

He pressed her hand. "I understand." He turned to Jake and waited while Dani made the introductions. "I hope we'll be seeing more of you, Mr. Rabb."

"Jake's just visiting," Dani said quickly.

"Of course." With one more look divided between the two of them, the minister left to visit with other members.

"How long have you known him?" Jake asked as they walked back to the car.

"Years. In fact, I can't remember when I didn't know Dr. Oleson."

"You didn't include him on the list."

"You can't seriously believe he's involved." Her voice rose in incredulity. "He's a minister."

"Priests were among those who testified against Christ," Jake reminded her. "You can't exclude anyone." He paused, letting that sink in.

Her earlier joy in the morning's service evaporated under his suspicions. "This monster is stealing my life, making me suspect everyone, even a man I've known since I was a child."

Jake held the door open for her. "I'm sorry. I know it's hard."

He didn't know how hard, she reflected with a droop of her shoulders. "Please take me home."

That evening, Dani retired early, more discouraged than she could ever remember being, even in those dark days following her mother's disappearance.

"Dear Lord," she prayed. "Please give me faith. My own seems to be missing in action."

FOUR

Dani awoke with a surge of optimism and a determination to live this day with courage and faith. She refused to let the monster who was stalking her control her life.

"You can't change yesterday and you don't know what tomorrow will bring. Live today." Those were among the last words her mother had said to her.

So when Victor Wingate called early Monday morning with an invitation to lunch, she accepted.

"Gordy's will be fine," she said, naming one of Atlanta's popular eating spots. At the same time, she ignored Jake's scowl. "Noon. I'll see you then."

She put down the phone and lifted her chin at the censure she read in his eyes. "I can't stop living just because some crazy person has me in his sights. All he's done is try to frighten me. If I change my life, he wins. I'm not going to give him that satisfaction."

Jake scowled. "I'm going with you."

"Fine. But keep your distance. I won't have you scaring Victor."

Jake didn't answer. He'd made his feelings about Victor plain, without saying a word.

It was true she had ended things with Victor, but he'd been a good friend, one she had grown to depend upon, especially in those first horrible weeks following her mother's disappearance. He'd held her hand, both literally and figuratively, during the long hours of waiting by the phone, praying for a word, something, anything, to tell them what had happened.

When the days had stretched into weeks, the weeks into months, she'd finally accepted that she was not going to find the answers she needed. It was then that she had realized what had happened with Victor.

She had mistaken gratitude for love.

In the ensuing years, they'd reclaimed much of their lost friendship, for which she was thankful. She didn't have so many friends that she could afford to lose one.

She worked through the morning with Jake doing research on the computer. He interrupted her only rarely to ask a question or two about a name on the list she'd compiled.

"The secretary. Clariss Trenton. I can't find much about her. What do you know about her?"

Dani put down the yellow legal pad where she'd been making notes. "Clariss? She's quiet, tends to stay to herself, but she's a hard worker. We'd be lost without her around here." She slanted a curious look his way. "You can't seriously think she's behind all this?"

"I don't know. Are you close to her?"

"Not particularly, though I like her well enough. She's barely twenty-three, just out of college." Something in her tone alerted him.

"What is it?"

"A year ago, she asked me to falsify information on her application to law school. I refused. Things were tense for a while, then eventually smoothed over." Dani paused. "I think she has a boyfriend."

Jake made a note and then checked his watch. "We'd better be on our way if you're going to get to Gordy's by noon."

At Gordy's, Jake made sure he got a table where he could both see and hear what was going on between Dani and

Wingate. Though he'd met the man only once, he didn't like him.

His research showed that Wingate was a defense attorney who rarely lost a case. As he specialized in criminal defense, he was not popular with the Atlanta P.D. Nothing surprising there. There was nothing about him to raise a red flag, but Jake couldn't shake an uneasy feeling about the lawyer. Maybe it was the way he looked at Dani.

"I'm glad you have protection," Wingate said with a nod in Jake's direction.

"Your father was right about hiring someone, though I'd do anything for you. You have only to say so." He reached across the table to press her hand. "You know that, don't you?"

Dani squeezed his hand in response, grateful for his offer. "Of course I do. But you're not trained to act as a bodyguard, and I'd never forgive myself if anything happened to you." A shudder raced through her at the thought.

Jake disguised a laugh with a cough. Dani glared at him.

He picked up his cup of tea, content to sip it while Dani and Wingate ordered a full meal. Jake made no attempt to disguise the fact that he was listening in on their conversation, despite the warning looks Dani darted at him.

"I was delighted that you accepted my invitation," Wingate said. "It's been too long."

Dani smiled. "It has. Things have been crazy at the office, what with the cases I'm trying."

"And your stalker."

Her smile died. "Yes. And that."

"If you'd give me the word, I'd take care of you," Wingate said in a rush and moved his chair closer to Dani's. "You'd never have to worry about anything again. I make more than enough to take care of the both of us."

If the man had been paying attention, Jake thought, he'd have noticed that Dani froze at the suggestion.

"I like my job, and I'm good at it," she said evenly. "I would never think of leaving it."

"Dealing with all those lowlifes, it's probably that job that's turned someone into a stalker. I told you that no good would come of you taking it." A peevish note entered Wingate's voice. He continued to inch his chair closer to Dani's. Either he didn't notice that she backed away with every move he made or he chose to ignore it.

The man had no boundaries, Jake concluded. He didn't take the hints that Dani was so clearly giving.

She put down her napkin. "Thank you for lunch, Victor. I'd love to stay and chat, but I'd better get back to the office."

"To your job."

"Yes. To my job." She stood. "Please don't get up. Finish your lunch." She walked away without looking back.

Jake started after her, but not without a warning look in Wingate's direction when the man made a move to follow her.

Outside the restaurant, Dani was fuming. "I remember now why I broke it off with Victor. He delights in telling me what to do, always assuming that he knows best."

"He doesn't seem like the type who likes being thwarted," Jake observed.

"He's not." She left it at that.

Jake grabbed her hand. "C'mon. Let's take a walk."

"I have to get back to work."

"It's early. Let's grab a hot dog. I know a great place where they pile on the pickles and onions and chili."

"I just had lunch."

"You pushed some overpriced lettuce around on your plate. That's not lunch."

"No, it's not," she agreed. "A hot dog it is. But I think I'll pass on the onions and chili."

The hot dog was infinitely better than the fancy salad

she'd ordered at Gordy's. Perhaps it was the company, she thought, with a glance in Jake's direction. Blunt, bossy and irritating as he might be, he made her laugh, and he made her feel safe.

Truth be told, she wasn't exactly anxious to return to the office. Ever since word had gotten out about the stalking, everyone had been treating her like fragile goods, politely keeping their distance, but she felt the stares, the whispers behind her back.

She didn't blame them. No one was comfortable being around a victim, and she didn't like being one. She lifted her chin. No one was going to make her a victim. Whoever was stalking her had better watch out.

A child's laughter caught her attention, turning her gaze to a young couple, a little boy between them, walking down the sidewalk. Their joy in each other was unmistakable, as well as their love for the child. A fierce longing swept through her to have that for herself, even as she recognized that it wasn't likely, given her current situation of not having a man in her life or even a date in four years.

"They make a pretty sight," Jake said, echoing her thoughts.

She couldn't help noticing the way the sun reflected off his deeply tanned skin and picked out glints of hazel in his dark eyes.

He dabbed at her chin with his napkin. "Mustard."

He tossed the napkin away but reached out to caress her cheek, and she heard herself sigh. Felt him draw her into the shelter of his arms.

The sweetness of the moment lulled her into forgetting they were standing on a city sidewalk for all the world to see. Suddenly aware of where they were, she pulled away, appalled at her behavior. Her smile felt awkward, stiff, but she managed it.

"I've never been able to eat a hot dog like a lady." It occurred to her that, despite all the trials of the past few

weeks, she was happy. More, a lot of that happiness had
to do with Jake.

A frown crossed her face at the direction of her thoughts.
No, that wasn't right. It wasn't Jake. She wasn't dependent
upon a man for her happiness. It was simply the joy of being
alive, of knowing that she was doing a job she loved and
that she was making a difference with it.

Jake was there to keep her safe. Nothing more.

His deep, rich laugh made her spine tingle for no other
reason than she liked the sound. "Ladies don't eat hot dogs,"
he said. "At least not those from a sidewalk vendor."

"You're right. If Mama could see me now, she'd raise
her eyebrows and wonder where I'd been brought up." A
smile trembled on her lips at the memory of her mother's
lectures on manners.

"For all that, though, she loved me. I never doubted
that. Until—"

"Until she left."

Dani nodded unhappily. "Until she left." Unwillingly,
she felt her thoughts slip back to that time.

She shook the unhappy memories away and focused
on the present. "I shouldn't have accepted Victor's invitation." She squared her shoulders. "I knew—or I should have
known—what would happen. He never changes."

"He's the type who wants to tell others what to do and
expects them to obey. Or else."

Did Jake realize that he had described himself, as well?
she wondered. He and Victor had nothing in common other
than that both liked to tell her how to run her life. She kept
that to herself, knowing he wouldn't appreciate the comparison. It served as a reminder, though, to not become involved with a man who was too fond of giving orders and
expecting them to be obeyed.

"You know practically my whole life story," she said.
"What about you? Were you ever engaged?"

Jake hesitated. "Once upon a time, I thought there was someone special," he said. "I was home on leave and went to a buddy's engagement party. His fiancée's sister caught my eye. Made me feel like some kind of hero. I was flattered. She was the daughter of a diplomat, class all the way. Or so I thought. We dated for five months and fell in love." His smile was rueful. "I'd saved up every penny I could, borrowed some more and bought a ring. I planned to propose to her the night before I shipped out."

"What happened?"

"I did the whole thing—got down on one knee, gave her the ring. She laughed in my face, then told me she was slumming to teach her boyfriend a lesson. Turns out, they'd had a fight and she wanted to bring him to heel. I guess it worked, because they got married two weeks later.

"Once my ego got over being trampled into the ground, I figured I'd had a lucky break. We would have made each other miserable if she'd said yes."

As if to emphasize that it was no big deal, Jake picked up a bag of peanuts, paid for it and then held it out to Dani. "Want some?"

She couldn't repress a shudder. "No. Thanks. I'm allergic."

Immediately, he tossed the bag of peanuts into the trash. "I'm sorry." He slanted her a curious look. "Just how allergic are you?"

"Enough that I almost died when I was ten years old. It was at my grandmother's house. The cook had made brownies as a treat for me and put peanuts in them, not knowing I was allergic. I was rushed to the hospital, had my stomach pumped and was given a massive dose of epinephrine.

"I recovered, but I still remember my mother crying and praying over me. She wanted her mother to fire the cook, but Dad persuaded her it wasn't anyone's fault."

"I'm glad you told me." He checked his watch. "Time we got you back to the office and me back to my research."

"Is this what bodyguards commonly do? Research?"

"That and throwing ourselves in front of our clients and taking a bullet for them if necessary. All in the name of duty, of course."

He was teasing, but she didn't want to think of Jake being shot—for her or anyone else. The direction of her thoughts pulled her up short. She didn't care about him other than as another human being. That settled, she felt better.

"Hey, it's all right," he said quickly. "I was only joking."

"I know." But her voice came out very small.

Jake reached for her hand. "I didn't mean to scare you."

"I won't have you risking your life for me."

"I don't take unnecessary risks."

"I don't want you taking *any* risks," she said fiercely. "Not for me."

"I'll do my job…whatever it takes." The last was said with a quiet inflexibility that expressed more than the words themselves.

She knew better than to argue. Jake was an honorable man, one who did what he promised and didn't make excuses.

Again she was grateful to her father for hiring Jake. She thought of putting her feelings into words, then thought better of it. She was a job to him. Nothing more.

Her earlier pleasure in the outing evaporated. She threw the rest of her hot dog in the trash. "You're right. It's time to get back."

Their trip back to the office was subdued.

They worked through the afternoon with minimal conversation. The case against Jerry Brooks was coming together, if only his wife stuck to her guns. Stephanie Brooks had been beaten over and over by her husband, and each time she'd refused to press charges.

This time was different.

"You can do it," Dani urged the woman over the phone. "You can't go on as you have been."

"I know," Stephanie said. "I'm not letting him get away with it. Not this time. I'm so ashamed that I've let it go on as long as it has."

"You have nothing to be ashamed about. It's Jerry who should be ashamed."

"I keep thinking if I had done something different, he wouldn't have hurt me like he did. He kept telling me that it was my fault, that I made him do it."

"That's nonsense, and you know it." Urgency roughened Dani's voice. She had seen it too often, the wife embarrassed, ashamed of her husband's abuse and taking the blame. She couldn't allow Stephanie to heap guilt upon her shoulders. The woman deserved a chance at happiness.

"You're right, of course. I just never thought it would come to this." Tears turned Stephanie's voice husky. "When I took my marriage vows, I believed they were forever. My parents told me that it was a wife's duty to stand by her husband. When I left him, they said I'd failed."

Dani bit her lip, stilling the angry words that wanted to spill out. How many times had she heard similar things from other women, browbeaten into staying with an abusive husband by family members who should have known better? "You didn't fail. You did the best you could, stuck it out far longer than you should have."

"Thank you for that." Stephanie's voice took on new strength. "I couldn't have done this without you."

"You'd have done it. If not now, then at a different time. You're a strong woman. You deserve to be happy."

"I'm beginning to believe you."

"Believe in yourself," Dani urged. "Believe in the Lord."

They talked a few minutes longer before Dani reminded Stephanie of the court date.

"You were good with her," Jake said after Dani hung up.

Dani took a deep breath, exhaled it slowly. "Stephanie's been through so much. I've been close before in convincing her to press charges against Jerry, but she couldn't bring herself to follow through. Now she's doing it."

"Brooks has a nasty streak to him. Even if he isn't behind the stalking, he could still make trouble for you."

She wasn't afraid for herself. She could handle Brooks. No, her fear was for Stephanie, who had suffered at his hands. Instinctively, she said a silent prayer that she could be there for Stephanie as the Lord was always there for her.

Jake recognized the quietness that had stolen over her as she prayed, the peace that appeared on her face. He understood that prayer was an integral part of her life and respected her for it. At one time, it had been for him, as well. He knew a momentary pang of regret that prayer had no place in his life. Not any longer.

Abruptly, she stood, placed her hands on her desk. Authority suited her, Jake thought. She wore it easily but never lightly. "Brooks doesn't scare me. When someone stands up to him, he runs. Like all men who abuse women, he's a coward at heart."

"You're right about that. All the same, be careful around him. He's not above trying to get even."

"I'm beat," she said. "If it's okay with you, I'd like to take off."

Jake nodded.

The rest of the week passed uneventfully. No more letters or calls or unpleasant gifts. It was easy to believe that the threat was over.

Too easy, Jake thought. This type of thing didn't simply blow over. An awards ceremony scheduled for next Friday still loomed ahead of them. Try as he would, he couldn't convince Dani to cancel her appearance.

A week before the event, he tried once more.

"I don't care about the award, but I have to be there," she said. "I promised the mayor as well as the director of the shelter. Plus, it's for a good cause. Every penny raised goes to the battered women's shelter."

"You could send a donation."

"I will. But I still have to be there." She paused. "Jake?"

"Yes?"

"Do you have a tux?"

The hesitancy in her voice had him grinning. "Yes. I have a tux. Does that surprise you?"

"Frankly, yes."

"After I left the service, I had a couple of things I had to go to. Decided it was cheaper to buy a tux than to keep renting one." He'd deliberately downplayed his reasons for needing a tux. The truth was he'd been summoned to the White House to receive an award for valor. It was the last thing he'd wanted to do, but he'd attended and accepted the award on behalf of those men who had given their lives for their country.

Once home, he'd tossed the ribbon and medal in the bottom drawer of his dresser and hadn't looked at them since. A ribbon for losing seven of his men wasn't something he was proud of. Nor was it something of which he wanted to be reminded.

"Someday maybe you'll tell me the real story of how you came to have a tux. In the meantime, it makes things easier."

"I'll try not to embarrass you." He quirked an eyebrow at her. "You're bound and determined to go to this shindig?"

"Bound and determined," she agreed with a smile.

"You're a stubborn woman."

"So I've been told."

One week before the event, Jake had gone over the blueprints for the Center for the Arts, where the banquet was being held, arranged with Monroe for plainclothes cops to be present and, along with Shelley, had done a background check on the catering staff. He'd covered every base, and still he wished Dani would chuck the whole thing, stay home and split a large pizza with him.

He couldn't shake the uneasy feeling that he was forgetting something. A soldier quickly learned the art of preparation before battle or he didn't make it home.

"You're obsessing," Shelley observed in one of their meetings in the office located at the rear of the house. "You've done everything you can. Frankly, big brother, I'm impressed."

He ignored that and focused on her assertion that he'd done everything he could. "Everything except kidnap her and spirit her away from here." He wasn't above doing just that. The grimness in his voice had his sister turning a frown on him.

"You care about her."

"I'm paid to care about her." The words came out more clipped than he'd intended, but he didn't apologize. He needed to remind Shelley and himself that Dani was a job. That was all she was, all she could be. A job.

An inner voice called him a liar. He did his best to ignore it.

A woman like Dani deserved a whole man, not a broken-down soldier who had seen too many of the world's atrocities, who had spent too much of his life in the darkness.

Shelley's frown deepened. "It's more than that, and you know it." She paused. "I know you don't like remembering Libya, but it might help to talk." She made a face. "I get it. You're this big, bad Delta Force soldier who doesn't like to share his feelings, but it doesn't hurt to talk about it sometimes."

She was wrong. Talking about that time in his life would

not help. Jake had long ago accepted the bad and the good and had learned to work with both.

"It's my butt on the line if anything happens to her. You said yourself that the senator is an important client. We can't afford to screw this up."

"He is." Shelley sighed. "I like your Dani very much."

"She's not 'my Dani.'"

Shelley only raised a brow. "Are you so sure?"

He ignored that. Shelley was a great sister, but she had a nosy streak a mile wide when it came to the people she cared about.

"I've got to go."

"Too bad I won't get to see you in your tux," she teased.

He gave her a gentle poke in the arm. "I'll fill you in on the evening later. If we're lucky, there'll be nothing to tell."

"If we're lucky," she agreed.

Jake had a feeling their luck was about to run out. In the army, he'd learned not to ignore the feeling that told him when something bad was coming down. That feeling was screaming now, warning him.

The only problem was he didn't know where the trouble was coming from.

FIVE

The whir of the ceiling fan disturbed the night air across Jake's body. Strangled breaths filled his chest.

Scenes too numerous to sort through flashed across his mind. Iraq. Afghanistan. Libya. The part of the world that had come to be known as the Sandbox by the special-ops community. All-nighters lying as still as death with a sniper rifle at the ready. Where he'd done what he'd been trained to do: stop the enemy in any way possible.

Somewhere along the way, somewhere between the killing and trying not to be killed, he feared he'd lost his soul.

He had seen things no man should see, things that had made him retch long after his stomach had emptied. Things like watching men die needlessly. Things like women begging for food to feed children who had gone too long without. He had listened to the dying gurgles of men, had heard the cries of women and children as they ran through streets as bombs exploded nearby.

All at once, he was in the huge cavity of the C-130 Hercules, stowing away the last of the team's gear. Dressed in desert cammies, light combat gear and Oakley assault boots, he made himself comfortable, or as comfortable as possible, in a thick mesh hammock.

Several hours before, his unit had been ordered to join SEAL Team Five for a joint operation. He must have been getting old, for the mission did not fill him with anticipation as it once would have. Instead, he felt only a terrible weariness.

The more terrorists they rounded up, the more that seemed to take their place. Insurgent groups filled with a fanatic hatred toward Americans and bent on killing American soldiers, no matter how many innocent civilians they wiped out along the way. He would never understand that careless disregard for life, the cavalier way the enemy considered what had been termed *collateral damage.*

His unit had been instructed to blow up an insurgent ammo dump. A routine mission. Or it should have been.

The loading ramp rose as the pilot fired up the mammoth turboprop freighter. The cavity of the beast filled with the rattle of horsepower and steel, making any conversation impossible.

Jake preferred it that way. The isolation caused by the unceasing noise gave him time for meditation and prayer. He never went on a mission without first praying. He knew the other guys didn't understand. Sometimes he didn't himself. When someone had seen as much as he had of men's depravity toward their fellow beings, it was hard to believe in the Lord and His goodness.

But despite what he'd seen, or maybe because of it, Jake had never stopped believing. So he uttered a simple prayer.

"Dear Lord, I know You are watching over Your children. Please bless us as we prepare for battle."

After a quiet "Amen," he let the steady roar of the Hercules's engine lull him into a light sleep.

Hours later, he and his men and members of the SEAL Team fast-roped down to their target. There was no reason why they should not secure the ammo dump, just as they had dozens of others in the past. Still, uneasiness filled Jake, making him hypervigilant as he scanned the area.

Everything looked as reported in the intel he'd read and reread.

When the first round of mortar hit, he knew his feelings had not been misplaced. Lightninglike streaks filled the sky. And, from the moment of one heartbeat to the next, chaos reigned.

"No, God. Please, no!"

Jake was hit, taking a bullet to his upper thigh. The burning pain brought him to his knees. A field dressing consisting of a strip of his undershirt hastily tied around the thigh was all he had been able to manage. He tried to stand, found that he couldn't, so he got on his belly and crawled.

The echoes of his men's screams cut through the night as Jake struggled to get to them. Enemy fire tore up the ground. Still, he tried to crawl over the pockmarked earth, dragging his useless leg behind him.

His Kevlar helmet, reminiscent of German World War II headgear, trapped the heat with stunning precision. Sweat streamed down his face, his neck. His backpack slowed him. He ignored both. He had to reach his men. Had to save them.

The distant *thump-thump* of their own Black Hawks promised help, but it was too late.

Much too late.

Artillery fire drowned out the shouts, and then there was nothing save moans and cries. Bile rose in his throat, the nasty taste of it sending waves of sickness through his body.

The ashen face of his best friend was mute evidence of his failure to protect his men.

At some point he must have lost consciousness, for when he woke, he was strapped to a gurney, being carried away, away from the destruction and devastation.

Sounds reached him, a voice begging him to wake up. The air held the stench of cordite and smoke and death. Death, he'd learned, had its own peculiar smell.

Despair filled him until, mercifully, he blacked out again.

When he awoke a second time, it was in a makeshift

hospital. Supplies were rationed, but he had rated enough morphine to keep the pain at bay. It was more than he'd expected, and he told himself to be grateful.

Instead, all he could think of was his fallen comrades, their blood spilled for a failed operation that never should have been attempted. Faulty intel had sent them into a war zone, outmanned and outgunned.

If only he'd listened to his gut. *If only.* Were there any words more useless in the English language?

Sweat pearled above his lip, trickled down his back. He thrashed around on the sofa, throwing off the lightweight blanket, then fell to his knees.

His friend's face morphed to Dani's. She lay among the bloodstained rubble, lifeless as a rag doll. Under the surreal and murky light of mortar fire and explosions, it was her eyes that stared at him. Her eyes that asked why he hadn't saved her.

A cry ripped from his throat. "No!"

"Jake!"

Hands gripped his shoulders, shook him gently.

He fought them off. Pushing away his attacker, he got to his feet, eyes huge, lungs pulling air like a bellows. The room spun around him. Was he back in Libya?

With a Herculean effort, he pulled himself from the nightmare. Breathless, dripping sweat, he surfaced. Only then did he recognize where he was. Reality returned in bits and pieces. Dani lay on the floor where he'd shoved her only a moment earlier.

He tried to answer the voice that called to him, but only a gaspy wheeze came out.

"Dani?" She didn't look hurt, only shocked. And no wonder. He had knocked her to the ground. Shame and revulsion at himself washed over him. What else had he done?

"It's me, Jake. Dani." Tentatively, she reached for him, and he automatically pulled her to her feet, drew her to him.

Small hands cupped his face, the palms soft against his skin. "Everything's all right."

He wanted to shout at her, to tell her that nothing had been all right since that day in Libya when he'd lost seven men.

Afraid that he might hurt her, he pushed her away. "You shouldn't be here."

"You brought me here, unless you forgot," she said, and he knew she was trying to make him smile, make him forget.

But he couldn't smile. And he would never forget.

"Where's Shelley?"

"She got a call from her client. She left a note on the kitchen counter."

Dani drew him back to the sofa, pushed him down and then knelt in front of him. "Tell me." She implored him with her expression.

"It's old news. It doesn't matter anymore." His breathing slowed as he took in his surroundings.

"Not when it has you screaming in the middle of the night."

"How bad was it?" he asked, unable to meet her gaze.

"Pretty bad," she said. "I thought someone had broken into the house."

"I'm sorry."

"Don't be an idiot. You were in pain. You're still in pain." Her hands gripped his. "Tell me what happened. Once you talk about your nightmares, they lose a lot of their power."

That was what the army shrink had said. The man had also said that Jake suffered from PTSD. Jake had dismissed that with barely concealed contempt. He was Delta Force. Deltas didn't have PTSD. He had a recurring nightmare. That was all.

"You've shut down your feelings," the psychiatrist had told him. "Once you start to feel again, you'll start to heal."

After that, Jake had refused to attend any more sessions with the man. Jake had had enough on his plate as he'd tried to rebuild his broken body. He didn't need any psychobabble from a shrink who had never seen battle.

What did some doctor who wore elbow patches on his jackets know about guilt?

The guilt was always there. Only his dreams loosed it.

"I did nothing but talk." The words came out as a growl, but she never flinched. "For months, I talked. To the army shrinks. To the chaplain. But it never did any good. Talk doesn't change anything. It never does."

"Maybe you weren't ready to face it yet."

"What makes you think I'm ready now?"

"I don't know if you are or aren't. But keeping whatever is torturing you locked inside won't do you any good." She spread her hands as if to encompass him, the room that still had not stopped spinning.

He supposed he ought to be grateful that the dream no longer came every night, but there was something even more horrible about its capricious visits, ambushing him when he'd let down his guard.

Strangely, he found he wanted to talk. To Dani. He started slowly, letting the memories have their way. "It was supposed to be a routine operation. A small unit would infiltrate a compound, lay down some explosives, then get out. My friend Sal and I took the lead. As soon as we were inserted, I knew something was wrong. The intel we received was faulty. They were waiting for us."

"They?"

"The Tangos. They were lying in wait, ready to pick us off one by one. Seven of us survived. Seven didn't. By the time I was shipped home, I was in a bad way. My leg…" He patted his right leg. "I was on crutches. But I could have dealt with that."

"Your men," she guessed. "You felt responsible."

"It was more than that. When I was able to, I did some digging. I learned that some congressman had wanted to score points with the media, told someone who told someone else about the operation. We lost seven men, seven good men, because some politician couldn't keep his mouth shut."

She gasped. "What did you do?"

"I resigned."

"You felt you had no choice."

"I didn't trust the bigwigs in Washington. I didn't trust my commanding officers. I didn't trust myself."

"Thank you."

"For what?"

"For telling me."

Jake scrubbed a hand over his face. "So you can live my nightmare with me? You don't need that."

"Did it ever occur to you that I need to be there for you, just like you're there for me?"

It hadn't. It shamed him that he hadn't given her needs a second's thought. "I'm sorry," he said for the second time.

"Don't be. You were hurting. I only want to help."

He doubted anyone could help, but Dani had made it clear that she wasn't going anywhere. He might as well answer a few questions. Maybe that would send her back to bed and he could deal with his pain by himself.

He was accustomed to dealing with things by himself. Preferred it that way. He'd been on his own since he'd enlisted. He'd been quickly singled out for the special-ops training and had excelled at everything they'd thrown at him. Riding high on the invincibility of youth and arrogance, he had believed he'd found his calling. He had a job he loved, and he did it well.

Then it had all come crashing down. He and Shelley never talked about his reasons for leaving Delta Force. His choice. He'd walked away with too many questions, questions that had no answers, at least here on earth.

"When you're ready to talk, I'm ready to listen," Shelley had said. He appreciated her patience, even as he accepted that he might never be able to talk about why he'd walked away from the service.

In the year since he'd left Delta, Jake had floundered, not knowing how to fill the days. A soldier, he was accustomed to action, whether it be slogging through relentless sandstorms, wading in putrid swamps or waiting out the night in teeth-rattling cold.

He hadn't been satisfied with his life since he'd left the military. He'd been in limbo, drifting day to day, without any sense of direction, so he'd jumped at Shelley's suggestion that they start their own security and protection firm, grabbing on to it as he would a lifeline.

He didn't need the money. Investing his salary over the years had paid off handsomely, and he would never have to work a day again in his life if he didn't want to, but sitting idly didn't come naturally to him. What he'd needed was a purpose.

Shelley, with characteristic stubbornness, had refused to accept any money from him. "Either the business makes it on its own or it folds. I won't take a dime from you, so don't even think about offering me a so-called loan."

They'd done okay so far, thanks to Shelley. He was content to leave the business end of things to his sister. He knew himself well enough to recognize that he didn't have the temperament for the boardroom. He also knew that he wasn't very diplomatic, if at all. He'd much rather kick a door down than talk his way in.

At thirty-five, he was in his prime, but too many years of fast-roping from helicopters and jumping from airplanes had taken their toll.

"What did you do when you came home?"

He grimaced. "Six months of physical therapy. I hated

every minute, but I didn't have a choice. Not if I wanted to walk again."

"I did some checking on you," she admitted. "Nobody's life is private anymore."

"That's only fair. I did some checking on you, as well."

"Now we're even." She paused. "How did you get through it? Being wounded, losing your men like that?"

He didn't want to talk about himself, but somehow Dani made him want to share with her. Only her. He wanted to share something real, not just the superficial things that men and women too often talked about. And it didn't get more real than this, the past that had made him the man he'd become. The good, the bad and, too often, the ugly. "I didn't. That's why I drag my nightmares along with me."

The anger roiling inside him threatened to erupt yet again, smothering everything else, so fierce and unforgiving that he trembled with the force of it. He fought it back, willed his mind to grow calm, but he couldn't vanquish the pain. It was all consuming.

A frown pinched her lips together. "Do you have them every night? The nightmares?"

"It's gotten better. Only once or twice a month now."

"What about the politician who compromised your mission? What happened to him?"

Bitterness twisted his face. "Nothing." The people who had first given the faulty information and the politician who had spilled the details of the op to the press had gotten a get-out-of-jail-free card.

Jake had railed against it, against the injustice of it. Every attempt he made to force the higher-ups into action against those responsible had been stonewalled.

The shrink the army had assigned to him told him that he needed to forgive.

Forgiveness didn't come easily. More, he didn't believe that the brass and politicians who'd sent his men to their deaths deserved his forgiveness. Frankly, they weren't worth the hard work he'd have to put into it.

Before he knew it, the feelings were pouring out of him.

Dani didn't try to talk him out of his feelings. Instead, she said only, "Forgiveness comes down to a choice. The Lord had to make a choice as well about whether to forgive the men who betrayed Him, who crucified Him. In the end, He chose forgiveness."

"You aren't comparing me to the Savior, are you?"

"No. None of us are worthy of that comparison. I'm only trying to say that forgiveness is within all of us, when we're ready." She hesitated. "You aren't going to tell me anything you don't want me to know, are you?" It was less exasperation that he heard in her voice than it was resignation. And regret.

"No."

"Then I should quit wasting my time." She started to get to her feet.

Jake grabbed her hand, pulled her back to the sofa. "I'm sorry." How many times was he going to say those words tonight? "I'm not good at sharing."

"I'm here to listen. When you're ready."

The Chicago projects where he and Shelley had grown up didn't make for warm and fuzzy memories, but they'd taught him to toughen up, and fast. It was strange; he hadn't thought of the projects in years. But the past was always with you, waiting to be reborn, to ambush you when you least expected.

He wondered what Dani would think of his background. It couldn't be more different from her own. Not that it mattered. Yes, the past was always with you, but you didn't have to let it define you.

Only the minister of a storefront church had shown any interest in a boy with more attitude than sense and his little sister. He had arranged babysitting for Shell while Jake worked, and he taught them both about self-respect and honor, hard work and reaching for a goal. Most important, the man had taught them that the Lord loved them, even when it seemed no one else did.

It was from attending that small church tucked away between a liquor store and a tattoo parlor that Jake had learned to pray. He'd thought his first attempts to talk to the Lord had been pitiful, but Reverend Weston had assured him that the Lord heard every prayer.

"The Lord doesn't care about fancy words. He cares about what's behind those words," the minister had said. "Chew on that for a spell. And don't ever tell me that you can't pray. Prayer is available to everyone. It's up to us if we take advantage of it."

Jake pushed away the regret that prayer was no longer part of his life and tore his attention from the past, back to the present, to Dani. He stood and drew her to her feet, as well. "Thank you."

Dani didn't ask what he was thanking her for. The press of her hands on his told him that she already knew.

He couldn't deny his wariness of his growing feelings for her. How could he? He had nothing to offer a woman like Dani. At the same time, he couldn't resist putting his arms around her. He wanted—needed—to absorb her goodness, her faith. His conflict was so great that he nearly pushed her away.

But he didn't. Couldn't.

For those moments, when he and Dani stood locked in an embrace, he forgot Libya and what had happened. He braced himself for the guilt that always followed whenever he forgot, even for a moment, the loss of his men, but it didn't come.

The following morning, Jake was remote, greeting her with only a grunt. Dani wasn't surprised, though she couldn't stifle a pang of hurt. He'd shared something important with her last night. Today, it appeared he regretted it.

"About last night—"

"Forget it," he said curtly. "I have." A shutter came down over his face, effectively blocking her out.

There was distance between them now on his part. And regret on hers. Disappointment had a sharp edge.

In a strange way, she felt betrayed. Why had he shared those memories with her, only to close her out hours later? Quietly, she reflected on the man who had so quickly become a part of her life.

There was more to this man than she'd guessed, and she wondered if he ever let anyone else glimpse behind the mask he wore with such determination.

"I'm going jogging. Then I've got some business to take care of," he said in that same brusque tone. "Shelley will stay with you until I get back."

Dani wasn't surprised that he was avoiding her and tried to convince herself that it didn't hurt.

Instinctively, she knew Jake wouldn't have shared what he had last night if he hadn't been hurting. Her heart squeezed tight, and she pulled a ragged breath into her lungs as she thought of him, a wounded warrior struggling to reclaim his life.

He was a true American hero. The arrogant man who had inserted himself into her life was only a facade.

While Jake took his jog, Dani took advantage of his absence and joined Shelley in the kitchen. The other woman was kneading bread dough, her hands capable and strong as they pounded it, then shaped it into a loaf.

"Go ahead," Shelley invited after she'd set the dough on a towel to rise. "I know you want to ask me questions about big brother."

Dani discovered she had dozens of questions about the

man who had insinuated himself into her life. Jake had become important to her in ways she wasn't ready to define.

Not yet.

"What was Jake like as a child?"

"Jake was never a child. Even before our mother cut out on us, he was taking care of me, making sure I did my homework, doing the cooking and cleaning. He had to grow up quickly."

Dani's heart hitched as she recalled the unemotional way Jake had described his childhood. There was no trace of self-pity in the recital, only an unaffected relating of facts that managed to reach down inside her. He'd made sure that Shelley knew she was loved. But who had loved the boy he'd been?

"That must have been rough. On both of you."

"Jake always made sure I had food and clean clothes to wear. Even when he went without."

Dani digested that. "He had a nightmare last night."

"Let me guess. Libya, right? His last mission?"

"Yeah. He told me a little about it."

"He told you?" Shelley's eyes widened. "He hasn't shared much with me, aside from the basic stuff."

Dani felt uncomfortable. "I'm sorry. I didn't mean to step on any toes."

"Hey, I think it's great. He needed to tell someone, to get the pictures out of his head. I hope he didn't scare you. Sometimes he wakes up screaming."

"He did," Dani admitted. Not for anything would she confess that she'd been scared out of her mind when she'd heard him shouting.

Shelley regarded her with a speculative gaze. "He must think you're pretty special, to share what happened in Libya with you."

"No. It's nothing like that. I was here. That's all."

"Did he tell you that he personally went to see the families of every man who died?"

"No. He said he spent some time in rehab."

"Six months. But he made time to visit every family, even when he could barely walk. He wouldn't have told me, but he needed me to drive him. That's the only reason I know. Otherwise, he'd have kept me in the dark."

Dani understood. Jake wasn't the kind of man to go around bragging about such a thing. He'd have kept it private. It only made her like him more.

"I thought you had a big case of your own. How did you find time to babysit me?"

"The bigwig I was hired to protect finally caved to the environmentalists' demands. The threat's gone and so am I." She wrinkled her nose. "I wasn't sorry to see the end of that job. The money was good, but the man was beyond obnoxious. Aside from that, he made a pass at me whenever he could."

Dani couldn't imagine anyone getting away with that and said as much.

Shelley laughed. "Oh, he didn't get away with it. The last time he tried, he ended up on the floor with my knee pressed on the small of his back."

Dani joined in the laughter. "Good for you." She bit her lip. "Could you show me a few self-defense moves?"

"Be happy to." Shelley stood, pushed a few pieces of furniture out of the way. "Let's start with a deflect and toss."

Dani went through the moves, using her shoulder to deflect the attacker, then rotating on her heels to toss him to the ground. By the time she had gotten the basics down, she was gasping for breath. Shelley, she noted, wasn't even breathing hard.

Shelley got up from the floor where Dani had tossed her. "I think that calls for a break."

"Thank you," Dani gasped.

Shelley laughed. "I worked you hard, but you did great."

"I'm going to practice on Jake when he returns."

Shelley gave her a probing look. "You like him, don't you?"

"Of course I like him. He's become a good friend."

Exasperation shone in Shelley's eyes. "I mean, really like him. The kind of like that happens between a man and a woman."

Dani suddenly busied herself studying the flowered design on her sweatshirt. "I don't know what you mean."

"I think you do."

To her relief, Shelley didn't pursue the subject, and Dani was happy to let it go. Falling in love wasn't in her plans. Love didn't mean a happy ending. Look at Jerry and Stephanie Brooks. They must have thought they were in love, at least at first.

She was wary of love, wary of the power it gave the object of that love over you. Yes, guardedness was definitely what she felt for Jake, among other more confused emotions.

She gave an exaggerated sniff. "I'd better hit the shower."

When Shelley suggested shopping an hour later, Dani jumped at the chance to do something normal.

They spent the next couple of hours at the Peachtree Mall. Shelley zeroed in on a pair of impossible-to-wear stilettos while Dani tried to decide between a cocktail dress in lipstick-red and one in black. Though she had suitable dresses, she wanted something new to give her confidence. "I've got this thing to go to at the end of next week," she confided.

"'This thing' as in the Georgia Benefits Award Night?" Shelley asked.

"How did you know?"

"I follow the news. I heard you were up for an award."

Dani made a face. "That's the last thing I want. But I

promised the director of the shelter I'd be there. It's for a good cause." She held up the two dresses. "Which one?"

"The red. Everyone will be in black. You'll stand out."

"I don't want to stand out."

"Honey, every woman wants to stand out. Besides, red is Jake's favorite color."

In the end, Dani decided upon the red dress, but only because it was on sale, she told herself. It had nothing to do with red being Jake's favorite color.

Nothing at all.

Jake knew he'd acted like a heel. He'd all but abandoned Dani. That he'd left her with Shelley wasn't the point. He'd known that Shelley would protect Dani with her own life, but Dani was his responsibility.

His reasons were not noble, not noble at all. Letting Dani see him in the throes of a nightmare was unacceptable. It made him vulnerable, and vulnerable was the one thing he could not be.

That was why he'd stopped going to the shrink. The doctor had labeled him as having PTSD. He had the occasional nightmare. No big deal.

And that was how he would treat the incident with Dani. As no big deal.

When he returned to the house, he found Dani in the front room, a pad of paper propped on her lap. She looked subdued, but the hurt was gone from her eyes.

"Hey, about earlier—"

"You needed a breather. I get it."

There was no reproachful scene as he'd feared.

"Yeah. I guess I did."

"I've got to work on my speech for next Friday. There's no time during the week. Not with everything else going on."

"About next Friday. There's no getting around it. It's a bad idea."

"I'm going, Jake. Please don't try to talk me out of it." She grabbed her papers and headed to her room.

It turned out that Shelley wasn't as forgiving as Dani. She tore into him when Dani left. "I don't know what's going on between you and Dani, but you better get your act together, big brother. Running out on a client isn't how S & J Security operates."

He could offer no excuse because there was none. "I blew it. I'm sorry."

"You should be." Her gaze softened. "You have nightmares. I get it. Just don't let them get in the way of the job."

Shelley had pegged it. He'd allowed a personal problem to interfere with the job. It was not only unacceptable; it was unprofessional. Deltas didn't desert a job because it got hairy.

Suck it up, he told himself, *and do the job.*

SIX

Shelley had been right.

The red dress made a statement. Dani did a little spin in front of the mirror, enjoying the flounce of the flirty skirt as it swirled around her legs. More, it gave her courage, and she needed an extra dose tonight.

She spent more time than usual with her makeup, playing up her eyes with smoky shadow and deepening her lips to a showstopping scarlet. The look was more dramatic than her everyday look, but she decided she liked the effect.

She'd tried to convince herself the threat was over, that the stalker had had his fun and had moved on, but she knew she was only fooling herself. She also knew Jake didn't believe the danger was over.

Things had been tense between them for a few days after the nightmare. She regretted that, just as she regretted Jake didn't trust her enough to share his nightmares with her. He'd made it clear that night had been a mistake.

Despite that, she trusted him, as much as she'd ever trusted anyone, aside from the Lord. The Lord had always been there for her and would continue to be there for her. Once the job was done, Jake would move on.

Not so the Lord. He was there to stay.

Whatever she felt for Jake was fleeting, temporary at best. It wasn't like her to give her heart to a man, any man. Occasionally she wondered if her reluctance to fall in love stemmed more from her feelings about her mother's abandonment than it did from her feelings about love itself. Was she allowing fear that someone else would leave her to rule her life and hold her hostage?

Acknowledging that she had never been in love with Victor, she had remained heart-whole since parting ways with him, and he had never roused the same feelings within her as Jake did. An impatient shake of her head should have cleared away the cobwebs that had taken up residence there. Instead, she felt more confused than ever.

Jake walked in at that moment. He was stunning in a conservatively cut tuxedo that showed off the breadth of his shoulders. A snowy-white shirt and black bow tie completed the look. The stark contrast of black and white enhanced his masculinity in subtle ways.

Before she could compliment him on his appearance, he bent his head and kissed her. Gently, so very gently. Softly, so very softly. And said, "Wow."

Wow, indeed. The kiss was gossamer light, a touch of butterfly wings, but it warmed her through and through. Wave after wave of longing flooded through her.

It was a kiss, nothing more. A barely-there kiss at that. She'd do well to remember why Jake was there.

He was a soldier, a man accustomed to action, even violence when necessary. They had nothing in common. When her stalker was found, Jake would take another job and move on.

With that self-administered dose of brutal honesty, she was able to put things in perspective and gave a small courtesy. "Thank you, kind sir, but you should thank Shelley."

"Why should I thank Shelley?"

"She convinced me to buy the red dress instead of the black."

"Remind me to thank her," Jake said fervently. "You look incredible."

"I wish I felt fabulous," she confided in a husky whisper. "You think something's going to happen tonight, don't you?"

"Your stalker's been quiet for over a week. Maybe it's over." But he didn't sound convinced.

"But you don't believe that."

"No," he said quietly. "I don't."

She stiffened her shoulders and her resolve. "Then we'll deal with it."

Jake lifted the jacket of his tux just enough to reveal the weapon he had holstered at his waist. "You're right. We'll deal."

She had no doubt that he'd risk his life to protect her. *Lord,* she prayed silently, *please keep Jake safe. I know everything, including our very lives, is in Your hands.*

Jake was silent, as if sensing her need for a moment of quiet. "You were saying a prayer, weren't you?" he asked quietly.

She wasn't surprised at his sensitivity and nodded. "Sometimes I need to talk to the Lord, even when it's not convenient."

Dani appreciated his understanding, especially knowing that he had his doubts. Jake's avowed lack of belief didn't ring true, and she wondered whom he was trying to convince—her or himself.

She turned her attention to the gun he carried.

Thanks to her father, who had one of the most extensive collections in the South, Dani knew her way around guns and could distinguish one weapon from the next. At various times, she had had to cross-examine policemen about their use of firearms and was grateful that she knew enough about them to ask the right questions.

Tonight, Jake carried a Glock. She recognized the automatic pistol and recalled her father saying at one time that the Austrian firm that manufactured the Glock had perfected the process of producing high-polymer handguns that could withstand the roughest treatment.

She watched as he strapped on an ankle gun, a Kahr P40. A whisper of a chill passed over her at what the guns represented.

"Are those really necessary?" she asked, then flushed at the stupidity of the question. Of course they were necessary.

"I think so." He drew her to him. "No one's going to hurt you. Not without going through me first."

It was absurd, but the protectiveness of his words gave her a rush of warmth. She was a job, she reminded herself, but Jake made it feel like more. Her pleasure in the words faded as she once more absorbed the significance of the guns he wore with such practiced ease.

The sight of the lethal-looking weapons, along with the grim note in Jake's voice, emphasized his worry about tonight. Perhaps she should skip the awards night and just stay home. Before the thought fully formed, she rejected it.

She had made a promise, and she wasn't going to break it. Tonight's event was to raise money for something in which she believed strongly. She wouldn't allow her stalker to steal the chance from her to make a difference for so many women.

She felt a vague embarrassment at her relief at Jake's solid presence. She was a grown woman who had been taking care of herself for years. She shouldn't rely on him, but knowing that she didn't have to face all this by herself felt good.

She held out a wispy shawl in gold mesh.

Jake placed it upon her shoulders. "The mayor's not going to thank you for this," he said.

"Why?"

"When people get a look at you, they'll forget he's even there."

That earned a laugh from her. "You're good for the ego."

"Just telling it like it is."

By the time they arrived at the Center for the Arts, Dani felt more in control and ready to enjoy the evening. Much of that had to do with the steady stream of light banter that Jake had kept up during the drive there.

"Stay close," he said when he escorted her inside the beautiful building. "I don't want you out of my sight. Even for a minute."

She nodded.

If Jake had thought they'd spend the night seated at a table, he was mistaken. Dani moved from one table to the next, stopping here and there to chat with people who were clearly enchanted with her. She was worth watching, he thought, a combination of grace, confidence and vitality.

The room was filled with the beautiful, the powerful, the influential. There was plenty of glamour and glitz, glad-handing and cheek-bussing.

In her red gown, Dani stood out as a flame. There were other women who were equally beautiful, he supposed, but the glint of purpose in her eyes set her apart.

Though he realized she was doing her part to raise money for the battered women's shelter, he wished she would stay put. It would have made his job that much easier.

When she finally took her seat at the head table, he drew a relieved sigh. As he'd done when they'd arrived, he scanned the room again with a practiced eye. Three exits. Discreet security guards at each. He'd filled in the chief of security about the threats on Dani's life, giving the man descriptions of Patricia Newton and Jerry Brooks for good measure, in addition to powwowing with Detective Monroe to make sure that undercover officers were also present. The detective had promised to be there, as well. "Dani's one of ours," he'd said simply.

They were covered, but Jake knew all too well how easily things could go south in an operation.

Background checks on the catering staff had not raised any red flags, though that didn't mean there wasn't a danger. An event like this was rife with opportunity for an attack. There were too many variables.

As the salad course was served, Jake's phone vibrated. With a glance at Dani that told her to stay put, he excused himself from the table and moved a few feet away.

"Jake."

He heard the anxiety in Shelley's voice. "What is it?" he asked.

"I was doing a second pass at the catering staff and found something. Patricia Newton was hired on for tonight."

"Why didn't we see that before?"

"She used her maiden name—Cahid. I should have picked up on it." Self-reproach filled her voice. "I'm sorry."

Jake went on full alert. "I'll get back to you." He hung up the phone without giving Shelley a chance to say more and hurried back to the table. He lifted the cover off Dani's plate and stared at the commonplace-looking salad.

"Don't touch it," he ordered.

By now, the security chief had moved in. "What's up?" Concern creased the man's forehead, digging grooves between his brows.

"Maybe nothing. But I don't want Ms. Barclay eating anything. I just learned that Patricia Newton is on the catering staff. It's no coincidence that she's here tonight. She could have slipped something into Dani's food."

To his credit, the man didn't bother asking a bunch of questions. Monroe joined them as well, barking out an order to one of the other men. "Stay with her," he said, pointing to Dani. "Don't let her out of your sight." He turned to Jake. "Let's you and me pay a visit to the kitchen."

In the kitchen, they found the head chef. "Patricia Cahid," Jake said. "Where is she?"

The rotund man shot them a harried look. "How should I know?" He waved a hand. "Out there."

Jake and the detective split up. When Jake spotted the woman, she was slipping out a side door. "Stop her."

The security guard stationed at the door detained her until Jake took over, clamping a hand around the woman's arm. "Going somewhere?"

"Let go of me." Newton tried to yank her arm free but couldn't break Jake's grasp. "I have done nothing."

"Then why are you leaving before the job's over?"

"I have a headache." She put a hand to her temple in a pathetic gesture.

By now, Monroe had joined them. "Let's take this somewhere more private," he suggested.

Jake saw they had attracted unwanted attention. He steered them into a cloakroom, then grabbed Newton's backpack. He rifled through it and came up with a small container. "What do we have here?" He sniffed. "Peanut oil." How would Newton know Dani was allergic to peanuts?

Her head came up. "So? It is not illegal to have peanut oil."

"Unless you happen to put it on Danielle Barclay's salad. She's allergic to it," he explained to the police detective.

Monroe pulled out a pair of cuffs and clamped them around the woman's wrists. "This is going to earn you another charge and likely more jail time."

Patricia Newton muttered something in a language Jake didn't recognize, but he had a pretty good idea of what she was saying.

"That was close," Monroe said.

"Too close."

They returned to where Dani waited. By then, a crowd had gathered around her. "What's going on?" she asked.

"You're going to have to skip dinner," Jake said.

Monroe took her plate and signaled to one of his men, who took it away. "We'll check it out. If we find peanut oil—and I think we will—Newton's going away for a long time on another charge of attempted murder."

Dani had gone pale. "Peanut oil. Why didn't I smell it?"

"The spices in the dressing masked it," Jake said. "We need to get you home."

She shook her head. "I'm staying."

"No way."

"You've already foiled the plot," she pointed out and would have made him laugh with the old-fashioned phrase if he hadn't been so worried. "I'm safe now."

"Just because we've stopped one thing doesn't mean there isn't something else."

She lifted her chin, a gesture he was coming to recognize. Though she remained sitting, she had a quiet air of authority. "I have a speech to make."

"What time are you on?"

"In forty-five minutes."

He helped her up. "Come on."

"Where're we going?"

"To get you a hot dog."

"A hot dog. Is that your cure for everything?"

"What's yours?"

"Prayer," she answered promptly. "Prayer is the ultimate protection."

Jake ignored that and, taking her hand in his, headed to the kitchen. "Let's see what the chef can fix up for us."

In the end, they didn't have hot dogs but managed to convince the chef to fix sandwiches for them after explaining the circumstances.

"On my staff? A murderer? It is not to be believed!" The volatile man was nearly apoplectic upon learning that Newton had finagled a job with his catering staff.

"No one's blaming you," Jake reassured him, for what seemed like the twelfth time. "But I'm sure you can understand that Ms. Barclay doesn't feel like eating anything the woman might have contaminated."

The chef personally prepared sandwiches, piled high with fresh vegetables and slices of meat and cheese. "May you enjoy," he said, presenting it to her with a flourish.

"Delicious," Dani told him. "Thank you."

He bowed from the waist. "It is my pleasure. Now, if you will excuse me, I must return to my work." He left, muttering under his breath about murderers, poison and the price of truffles.

It was time for them to get back to the main hall, as well. "Are you sure you're up to this?" Jake asked. Worry creased his brow and settled into his eyes.

"I have to be. I gave my word."

For Dani, he knew, that said it all. Her word was everything, and, with that, he felt the bond between them grow stronger.

He escorted her to the stage, then took a place at the left side where he could watch both her and the audience. True, they had caught Newton, but he still didn't feel that the woman was behind the threats. She had seized an opportunity and used it to her advantage, using her favored method of poisoning—in this case, peanut oil.

Newton had a craftiness about her, a native cunning, but she lacked the intelligence to plot the series of events that had plagued Dani. Jake's thoughts drew to a standstill as he wondered if he didn't want Newton to be guilty of the stalking, because, if she were, that would mean his job was over.

Self-honesty demanded that he admit he wanted to spend more time with Dani. He recognized the irony of that. He hadn't wanted the job, and now he wasn't ready to give it up.

What was going on with him? His feelings for her were causing him to doubt himself. He'd already allowed them to interfere with his ability to do his job when he'd left Dani with Shelley.

The strict professionalism he'd always brought with him to a job was conspicuously absent when it came to Dani. Having feelings for a client wasn't like him, but a lot of things he did lately weren't like him.

He turned his attention to the front of the room, where Dani had the audience eating out of the palm of her hand. She managed to achieve just the right tone, outlining the plight of abused women and their children while appealing to the listeners' compassion.

Her reaction to all that had happened was more than admirable. Courage under attack was something any soldier quickly learned to appreciate. Dani had that and more. She'd exhibited a kind of grace under fire that defied description. She might be wounded from the threatening letters and packages, but the stalker hadn't succeeded in breaking her.

The hearty applause following her speech was evidence that she'd succeeded. The mayor appeared at her side and presented her with the Humanitarian of the Year award.

"Thank you, Mr. Mayor, but I don't deserve this award. It should go to the women who have the courage to change their lives. With that in mind and your permission, I'd like to give it to the shelter, where any woman who seeks sanctity there can see it."

More applause. The audience couldn't get enough of her. Jake didn't blame them. Dani was both gracious and generous in her praise of others.

Impatiently, he waited while Dani stopped to accept congratulations from the dozens of people wanting to capture her attention.

"You were wonderful," a blue-haired matron told her. "You can count on my support."

Dani hugged the older lady. "Thank you, Mrs. Stanley.

We need more people like you." When Mrs. Stanley left, Dani yawned widely, then clamped a hand over her mouth. "I'm sorry. I think everything is catching up with me."

Jake had had enough. "That's it," he said when she was waylaid yet again. "You're exhausted, and this monkey suit is strangling me." He had already loosened his bow tie.

She gave a tired smile. "You're right. I am exhausted. But you look awfully good in your monkey suit."

Dani didn't have to be convinced to go home.

By the time they left the Center for the Arts, Jake was half carrying her to the car. When they reached his house, she was nearly asleep. The events of the evening plus the stress of the past weeks had caught up with her. She was not only physically weary; she was emotionally bruised.

In terms of raising money for the shelter, tonight had been an overwhelming success. It was less so in terms of her own well-being. The idea that someone hated her enough to try to kill her was only now sinking in. She felt chilled, inside and out. Her stomach twisted in hard, painful knots.

Outside, a spring storm raged, lightning flashing and thunder sounding its fury.

Lord, she prayed, *please let me weather this storm, too.*

At the house, she ran for the bathroom, fell by the toilet and emptied her stomach of its contents. She retched until only dry heaves were left, leaving her trembling. She couldn't stop shaking. Only then did she notice that Jake was there, holding her hair back from her face.

Embarrassed that he should see her this way, she tried to turn away, but he shifted his hands so that they framed her face. "Don't be embarrassed. And don't beat yourself up for being human. You held up better than most after what you've been through."

He helped her up, then steadied her as she washed her

face and brushed her teeth. She felt marginally better and started to head out of the bathroom when Jake swept her into his arms once more.

He carried her into the living room and gently laid her on the sofa. There, he worked her feet out of her high-heeled sandals. "I don't know how you women wear these things. They look like some kind of medieval torture device."

She sighed. "That's better. And you're right. They are torture devices."

Jake did away with the bow tie to his tux and shed the jacket.

"I want to be there when the police question Newton," Dani said. "We need to find out how she knew about my allergy."

"Who else knows about it?" Jake asked.

She gave another sigh, this one more resigned than tired. "My father, of course. Some friends. My coworkers."

He frowned. "That doesn't narrow it down much, does it?"

"No." Her frown matched his own. "Does it matter? You caught her. She's in custody, and if I have anything to say about it, she won't make bail. Not this time."

"Think about it, Dani. Newton had to learn somehow, somewhere, what peanut oil would do to you. Someone had to tell her."

Her thought processes were sluggish as she struggled to put things together. "You think someone used her."

"That's exactly what I think."

"Then it's not over." She didn't make a question of it, and he didn't treat it as such.

"No." He brushed a strand of hair back from her face. "It's not over."

And, suddenly, it was all too much. Tears trickled down her cheeks, and her shoulders shook. "I don't know how much more I can take."

Jake sat beside her, pulled her into his arms. "I'm still here. And I'm not going anywhere."

She clung to him. "Thank you. You probably saved my life tonight."

"Aw, shucks, ma'am. It's nothing any red-blooded American wouldn't have done."

How did he always know what she needed? "That's what you are—a real, honest-to-goodness red-blooded man."

Jake tipped an imaginary hat and winked. "Thank you kindly, ma'am. We red-blooded men do our best."

"And we damsels in distress appreciate it." The light-hearted banter lifted her spirits momentarily before the reality of her situation settled in once more. Someone wanted her dead.

"I'm going to turn in." She stood. "See you in the morning."

Jake pressed a kiss to her forehead. "We'll get through this."

She held on to that promise like a drowning man grabbed hold of a life preserver. "I know." She paused. "Thank you. For everything."

After a restless night, Dani rose, determined to work, even though it was Saturday.

"Don't you ever stop?" Jake asked.

She looked up from her laptop, where she was making notes on a case. "Not when I have seven cases needing my attention." Her eyes took on a fierce light. "And with Newton's little trick last night, that makes eight."

Jake's cell phone buzzed. He answered and listened, nodded to himself, listened some more. "That was Monroe. He asked if I wanted to sit in on questioning Newton."

"I want in."

"And I want you to stay put. Shelley will stay with you."

"You mean babysit me."

He didn't bother to sugarcoat it. "Yeah. I mean baby-sit you."

"Newton tried to kill me. I should be in on the interrogation."

"Each time you step out of this house, you're a target." Jake's voice turned persuasive.

"If it were you who was being targeted, would you allow someone else to question a suspect without you being there?"

She had him there. She could see it in his eyes. "All right. But you do what I say, when I say."

Dani sketched a mock salute. "Yes, sir." The words were light, but the tone was not.

Monroe met them in the squad room, gestured to a corridor. "Back there."

Jake and Dani followed the police detective into an interrogation room and settled into the chairs the detective indicated.

Newton was already there, cuffed and throwing off vibes of hatred. Small, mean eyes raked Jake and Dani contemptuously. A curtain of greasy hair fell across her face. "Why is he here? He is not police."

"I invited him," Monroe answered.

Newton's lawyer, a stocky, dark-eyed woman, spoke for the first time. "My client has rights."

"Yes," Newton piped up, her gaze snapping up to meet Monroe's. "I have rights."

Monroe clenched and unclenched his fists. "You have the right to answer my questions."

A sly look entered Newton's eyes. "I will answer questions. But I must have something in return."

"What do you want?" Dani spoke for the first time.

"Immunity," the lawyer answered for her client. "My client will answer your questions for immunity."

"Forget it," Jake growled.

Dani shot a warning look at him. He had no official standing. "No deal," she said.

"I have information. Important information." Newton looked from one to the other, her expression shrewd and assessing. "You," she said to Jake. "You have feelings for her. You want to know how I knew about the peanut oil?"

"I want to know, yes," he said, ignoring the reference to any feelings he might harbor for Dani.

"Then you must give me something."

He searched her face for a hint of remorse, but found no sorrow that she had tried to kill another human being. What had he expected? She'd already tried to murder an elderly man. Taking another life would hardly faze her. Her cold-as-death eyes reflected a soul totally devoid of normal feeling. What turned an individual so completely away from good?

He wanted to feel some kind of compassion for her but could find none within him and hardened his heart. "I can't make deals," he said before Dani could answer for him.

"No. But you can convince her that she should trade. You're some kind of bodyguard. She will listen to you." Newton's face twisted into a sneer. "Her kind always listens to a man."

Jake made no attempt to hide his contempt for the woman.

"*She*," Dani said with quiet emphasis, "can speak for herself. As I said—no deal."

Newton twisted a strand of hair, a careless gesture that grated on Jake's nerves.

They were at a stalemate. Jake knew it. Dani knew it, as well. Her motions coldly deliberate, she closed her briefcase, pushed away from the table and stood. "We're done here."

"Ms. Barclay." The lawyer stopped her. "My client has

valuable information to trade. As this directly affects you, I think you should resign from this case."

The prim speech did nothing to endear the woman to Jake.

It was Monroe's turn to weigh in. "Your client tried to kill the deputy district attorney and you want us to give her a deal? No way."

"You will be sorry." It was Newton who spoke this time. Was that desperation in her voice? She must know that she faced heavy charges with equally heavy sentences attached. The woman had a well-developed sense of self-preservation and made one last attempt. "I am foreigner here, yet you put me in cell, treat me like I am nothing." Fat tears rolled down her cheeks.

Crocodile tears, Jake thought, without an ounce of sympathy for what the woman was facing.

Jake and Dani followed Monroe from the office.

"She's got something to trade," the detective said. "But it sticks in my craw to deal with scum like her. She'd sell her own children for the right price." Monroe paused and directed his next words to Dani. "I didn't expect you to cut a deal with someone like Newton, but we might be missing a good bet."

"No."

"Even if it means finding out who's out to hurt you?" Jake had to ask. He respected her integrity, but he couldn't dismiss a chance to solve who was behind the stalking.

"Even if." She waited a beat. "Would you?"

He didn't answer right away. He was too busy taking in the picture she made. She was magnificent. Her slim body was warrior-straight; her chin lifted in determined defiance, her dark red hair tucked behind her ears, but it was her eyes that captured and held his attention. They challenged him to convince her that she was wrong.

He couldn't. "No. I wouldn't." The admission didn't come easily to him, but he refused to lie to her.

It wasn't the first time she'd turned the tables on him. He didn't appreciate it, but he couldn't fault her for her feelings, not when he'd have done the same.

She faced him squarely. "If I stepped back from this, if I didn't do everything I could to get justice for Mr. McBride because of some threat to me, I'd never be able to trust myself again, to believe in myself. If I don't have that, I don't have anything." Her eyes willed him to understand. "It's a matter of ethics. Without that, I don't know who I am."

He wasn't surprised. Her job, upholding the law to the best of her ability, defined Dani. Being under attack, in her eyes, didn't compare to the attempted murder of an elderly man.

"Before my father was a senator, he was a judge. I asked him how he always knew what was right. He said, 'It's more important to do right than to be right.'" She brought her hands to his wrists. "I have to know what I'm doing is right. We'll get the information some other way. We'll subpoena her phone records, go through her financials. Chances are she got some payoff, and it'll show up somewhere. Money always leaves a trail. She's not one to do anything without being paid for it."

Jake nodded. The woman was motivated by greed that trumped even her need for revenge. "What do you want to do?"

"Exactly what I said. Find another way to get the information." Dani's voice had gone hard. "I won't trade Mr. McBride for whatever crumbs Newton deigns to give us. She tried to kill that poor old man. He deserves justice. And he'll get it."

Jake's admiration for Dani rose another notch. The woman had more guts in her little finger than many hardened soldiers whom he'd fought alongside. At the same time, he was scared. For her.

Newton's stunt took things to the next level. Perhaps Dani didn't realize it, but he did. He was charged to protect her, to put an end to the stalking. And she was charged to refuse the very thing that could help him do just that.

He understood, but didn't agree. Even as they worked toward a single goal, their individual needs—his to protect her and hers to get justice for a victim—set them at cross-purposes.

Conflicting emotions roiled through him, tempting him to want to bundle her off where he could keep her safe from all harm, and he knew if he did, she would hate him for it.

Never before had a client's feelings interfered with the job as they did now.

At the house, Jake filled his sister in on what had transpired.

Shelley listened, then spoke for the first time. "Seems like you've got another avenue to pursue."

"What's that?" he asked.

"Take your list of the people who knew about Dani's canary when she was a child. Cross-reference it with anyone Newton's had contact with in the last couple of weeks."

"That's good, baby sister. Really good."

"Thank you, big brother." Shelley stood. "Now, if you two will excuse me, I'm going to hole up in the den. I've got some bids I want to get out."

"Thanks. I owe you."

"That you do." She tapped his cheek with sisterly affection. "And be sure that I plan to collect."

With Shelley's departure, much of the energy vanished from the room. In its place was a kind of tension.

Jake didn't mistake it as tension resulting from the stalker situation. This was different. It was the kind of tension that grew between a man and a woman. He had only to think of Dani to feel the awareness that had been there from the first time he'd laid eyes on her.

The wariness in her eyes, mixed with undisguised warmth, gave evidence of her own feelings. There was only one problem. She was a client he was assigned to protect. In his experience, mixing business and personal was never a good idea.

Never.

So he kept his feelings to himself. Dani had already seen him weak and vulnerable, thrashing about in the grips of a nightmare. She didn't need to learn more of just how broken inside he was. She deserved better. Much better.

Despite her job, she lived in a world full of light. His was colored by the darkness of his past, starting with the abandonment of a father he had never known and a mother who had discarded her children with no more thought than she would give a used tissue.

His days in the army had only confirmed his belief that the world was a harsh, unforgiving place. Nothing he had seen had convinced him to think otherwise. What if he were to take a chance with Dani? He'd only drag her down into his world. He'd die before he'd do that.

To his relief, Dani seemed no more inclined to give voice to the attraction that existed between them than he did.

As if sensing his need for a diversion, Dani pivoted on her toes and raised her leg high in the air, aiming a foot in his direction. She took him by surprise.

She missed his chest by a hair. "Shelley's been teaching me some self-defense moves."

He grinned. "Not bad."

They went through a series of moves with Jake offering suggestions to refine Dani's technique. She was never going to have the strength to take down a man twice her size, but she could learn how to defend herself enough to escape if someone should grab her.

"Enough," he said when he noticed that she was panting with exertion.

"I need to bulk up," she said. "I'm puny. You're just too polite to say it."

"No one's ever accused me of being polite. Besides, I think you're a cute kind of puny."

Dani grinned. "Good save."

"There's something I was to run past you."

She waited.

"I want to bring in a buddy from Delta. With two of us, we can do a better job of covering you."

"You're doing a great job," she said staunchly.

"It shouldn't have gotten as far as it did with Newton." Self-recrimination was heavy in his voice.

"Who is this buddy?"

"His name's Salvatore Santonni. He's a good soldier, an even better friend. I'd trust him with my life." He paused. "And with yours."

"If you think we need him, do it. I want this over." She shook off the grim mood that had settled over her. "What about ordering Chinese? I feel in the need of empty calories and MSG."

"Good idea." He picked up his phone and ordered from his favorite Chinese restaurant. "Hope you're hungry. I ordered enough to feed a small third-world country."

"I'll do my best."

The food arrived within a half hour. By that time, both Jake and Dani had showered and changed. After Dani offered a prayer upon the food, they attacked the white cartons with relish.

"Mmm. Spiced shrimp," she said, digging into the shrimp-and-vegetable concoction. "My favorite."

"Save some," he ordered, "or I won't share the spring rolls."

"You've got yourself a deal." Her good mood took a

nosedive. "You think I should offer Newton a deal, don't you?"

"It's like you said—we'll find another way to find out how she knew about the peanut oil."

Dani took a pull on the bottle of soda he handed her. "Making a deal goes against everything I believe in. Even when it's necessary."

"So we'll make sure it isn't necessary this time."

She forked up a piece of shrimp. "My boss isn't going to like it. Neither is the senator."

"Why do you refer to your father as 'the senator'?"

"Old habit. When I was growing up, he was always larger-than-life. He was gone a lot, and when he came home, he filled the house with his voice, his energy. I loved that about him. I still do. But he can be overwhelming." She wrinkled her nose. "Especially if he doesn't get his own way."

"You have a lot in common."

"How do you figure?"

"You're both smart and stubborn. You both like your own way. You both fight for what you believe in. Neither of you will give an inch when you believe you're right."

She dipped her head in acknowledgment. "You're right. The only difference is I don't try to tell him how to live his life. Ever since my mother disappeared, Dad hasn't been the same. He's terrified something will happen to me. If he had his way, he'd wrap me in cotton wool and stuff me away in the attic."

"You can't blame him for wanting to keep you safe. I imagine I'd feel the same if I had a daughter."

"I don't blame him. I just wish he'd trust me to know what I'm doing. I can't be the pampered princess he wants to make me." She arched a brow in his direction. "The spoiled princess you thought I was when you took this job."

"I was wrong," he said promptly. "You're no spoiled princess." The more he learned about Dani, the more he realized she was a mass of contradictions, a curious blend of wariness and emotion, strength and vulnerability.

"When did you change your mind?"

"When you saw that dead bird and didn't flinch."

That wasn't all, of course. There was a lot to like about Dani, he reflected. He appreciated the closeness that had grown between them, the total acceptance she gave him even when she didn't agree with him, especially about matters of faith. But most of all, he cherished the lack of loneliness she brought him. No one else, not even Shelley, had been able to penetrate the walls he'd built around himself since Libya.

Dani had made herself an important—too important, perhaps—part of his life. He would do well to remember that she was a client. Nothing more. He frowned at the direction of his thoughts. How many more times did he have to give himself that particular pep talk?

As many as it took, he thought with harsh resolve. Dani didn't need an ex-soldier in her life, broken in both body and spirit. She needed someone who lived in the light, not a man who had spent too much of his life in the shadows.

Once this was over, she wouldn't need him at all. The bleak thought brought him no comfort.

SEVEN

Newton didn't get her deal.

"She'll stand trial for both charges of attempted murder," Dani said in satisfaction after a meeting with the D.A. on Monday morning. "If I have my way, she'll be going away for a long time."

Jake knew Dani's own case mattered far less to her than that of the man Newton had tried to poison. Dani wanted justice for him.

Wanting justice was the reason why Jake had enlisted in the army—that and the need to protect the innocent. Much youthful idealism had been stripped away from him, but he could still feel glimmers of it now and again.

It was refreshing to see it in Dani, to watch her fight for those who could not fight for themselves. She was a warrior every bit as much as any soldier.

When he said as much, he was surprised to see tears fill her eyes. He hadn't expected to make her cry.

"I'm sorry," she said. "It's just good hearing that. I wondered if anyone understood why I do what I do. That I'm trying to make a difference."

And wasn't that another reason why he'd enlisted? To make a difference? To protect a way of life that was more precious than life itself? In his experience, that desire burned brightly in the men and women who served their country.

Jake believed. He believed in himself. He believed in

his skills. He believed in the country that he'd spent most of his adult life defending.

Dani's quest for justice rekindled that belief, despite what he'd been through. And maybe, just maybe, he thought with a start, her belief in God had sparked his own.

He pushed that away. God hadn't been there for his men. Why should he, Jake, believe that God cared what happened to him?

Whatever his feelings about God, however, he respected Dani's belief, respected what she was trying to do. "You *are* making a difference. Look at what you're doing for Stephanie Brooks. If not for you, she'd still be a punching bag for her husband. You've given her a new chance at life."

"Thank you. I needed that." She sounded vulnerable, and all of his protective instincts came out.

"You could have taken the easy way, given Newton the deal she wanted. No one would have blamed you. But you stuck to your guns. That takes guts. And courage. Never let anyone tell you differently."

"I couldn't go back on my word to Mr. McBride and his family. They've been through so much. Patricia Newton is going to pay for what she did. It won't make things right, but maybe it will be some satisfaction."

Jake wanted to kiss her, right there in the middle of the D.A.'s office, with her colleagues moving from one office to the next, with the phones buzzing and the whir of the copier an uneven counterpoint.

He could only imagine her reaction should he put thought to action. She'd be shocked, perhaps even horrified, but he couldn't help wondering if there'd be a tiny part of her that was thrilled.

At times he thought Dani had feelings for him, or maybe that was just wishful thinking on his part. Abruptly, he pushed those thoughts away. He had no business thinking of Dani that way. His own past had left him distrustful of the idea of love. He had no experience with it, no example from parents who had loved each other and their children. What did he know of giving or receiving love beyond that of a sibling relationship?

Nothing.

Over the years, he'd watched several of his friends fall in love and have the requisite white wedding, only to have the marriage end in bitterness and hatred. He didn't want that. Better to keep his heart safely tucked away, free from pain and loss.

He drew in a harsh breath and struggled to remember what they'd been talking about. Patricia Newton. That was it. "What happens next? With Newton."

"Her lawyer will push for a change of venue. She may get it, seeing as I'm the prosecuting attorney as well as a victim. I'll argue against it."

"Will you win?"

"I plan to."

"How long does a trial of this type usually take?"

She pursed her lips. "With jury selection, the trial itself—anywhere from three weeks to a month."

"And you still have the rest of your caseload to deal with."

She pushed up the corners of her mouth and managed a smile. "We don't have the luxury of working on only one case at a time around here. We're spread thin enough as it is."

"I know. I've seen your caseload."

"I'm not the only one. We all have similar caseloads." Her mouth drooped, her earlier elation vanished. "Ryan's been pushing to get some of mine. He wants to make a name for himself."

"Is that normal, for an A.D.A. to poach on a colleague's cases?"

"It's not abnormal. Like I said, he's ambitious. It goes with the job."

"What about Sarah? Does she poach, as well?"

"Sarah doesn't poach so much as she steps in to take credit for other people's work. We all know it, even Freeman."

"And yet you give her a pass."

"She does good work, when she has a mind to. Either she or Ryan could prosecute the case without a problem. They're each competent. They'd do the job."

"But they don't care the way you do," Jake said.

"No," she said softly. "Neither of them care the way I do. That's why I have to keep Newton's case. I owe it to Mr. McBride and his family."

"You'll run yourself into the ground if you keep this up." In the short amount of time he'd known her, he couldn't help but notice that she'd lost weight, that the shadows beneath her eyes had grown deeper, giving her a fragile appearance that made her look as though she would shatter into a thousand pieces at any moment.

"I don't know any other way to be."

No, she wouldn't, Jake thought. Dani gave her all and then some. She didn't have it in her to hold back, to let others pick up the ball because she'd been dealt a blow. He loved that about her. At the same time, it worried him.

She was under tremendous stress and would continue to be until her stalker was caught.

She couldn't afford to let down her guard. Neither could he.

A summons to Belle Terre was not to be ignored. Dani had sidestepped the last few invitations from her father, but she knew she could not get out of this one. He was worried about her and needed to be reassured. Knowing that his worry came from love helped take the sting out of her annoyance.

The familiar mixed bag of emotions fell heavily upon her shoulders, weighing them down, a confusion of love and longing, disappointment and misunderstandings. She just wished her father saw her as she was, a grown woman with a job she loved and was determined to do, with a life outside the mansion that had been home for her first eighteen years of life. Though she loved him dearly, she would not submit to the kind of smothering attention and protection that had been foisted upon her as a child.

Ever since her mother had disappeared four years ago, she and her father had been especially close. With that closeness, though, had come more of the overprotective tendencies he harbored.

So late Monday afternoon, she and Jake made the twenty-mile drive to Belle Terre. The sun blazed through the windshield, and she lowered her visor to block its piercing rays.

The greenery of the passing fields, the silhouettes of horses in the paddocks, the sheer openness of the sky were comforting, familiar and a stark contrast to the noise, pollution and congestion of Atlanta. She wondered what Jake thought as they put more and more distance between them and the city.

The houses no longer crowded each other as they had in town but had given way to land-rich estates that spread for miles. Only discreetly placed fences announced the boundaries.

When he turned the Jeep into the private lane to Belle Terre, Jake whistled. "You have your own road? Should I pay a toll?"

She gave his arm a playful slap. "Not until you reach the main house. Then a tribute and a tug of your forelock would be nice."

Dani expected him to laugh at that, but, instead, he only

said thoughtfully, "I feel like I've just stepped into an alternate universe."

She shot him a worried look. Was Jake like the few boys she'd dated in her teen years, intimidated by her family's wealth, their home, their name? She hadn't thought so, but more than one beau had dropped her after seeing her home for the first time. It hadn't helped that her father was a United States senator and had a gun collection that rivaled those found in museums.

Then she laughed at herself. Jake, a former Delta Force soldier, wouldn't be intimidated by something as superficial as a few acres and a house.

"What's so funny?"

"Nothing."

Belle Terre wasn't the largest home in Georgia, but it was one of the oldest and one of the last family homes to be passed down from generation to generation. Many of the South's older estates had been parceled out, piecemeal, to developers, to corporations looking for a country retreat for their top executives. Belle Terre remained, having survived the War Between the States, the invasion of carpetbaggers, the Great Depression and even a fire that had destroyed much of the upper level.

It had survived because of the determination of the people who had called it home. A fierce sense of pride filled her as she thought of her ancestors, especially the women, strong and independent and feisty as all get-out.

As a child, she'd spent hours at a time reading old diaries she'd found tucked away in a forgotten bureau in the attic. The stories she'd found there filled her with awe and a determination to never dishonor her family name.

Neither her grandmother nor her great-grandmother would have folded under the nastiness the stalker had seen fit to heap upon her. They would have shaken their fists at the world and dared anyone to try to frighten them.

A wave of sadness swept over Dani as she acknowledged that she couldn't say the same for her own mother.
Madeline Barclay had taken off, without even a goodbye,
much less an explanation. Determinedly, Dani shook that
off. She wasn't her mother.

She wasn't her grandmother or her great-grandmother
either. She was herself. Dani Barclay. That had to be good
enough.

She directed Jake to park the Jeep in front of the house.

"You sure about that?" he asked with a doubtful look at
the manicured lawns that flanked the drive, the carefully
tended flower beds, brilliant with color and texture, the
white-pillared porch. The front yard swept down from the
house like a velvet skirt in rich emerald. The setting sun
bathed the centuries-old white-brick mansion in pinks and
golds, giving it a fairy-tale appearance. "I feel like I should
be crossing a moat."

She laid a hand on his arm. "Belle Terre is just another
home."

"It is not just another home."

She supposed he was right, but it was home to her, though
she hadn't lived there full-time since she'd graduated from
high school. In some ways, it always would be home. It was
here she had learned to ride a horse, then drive her first
car. It was here that she had laughed with her mother when
they spent a summer afternoon trying on old clothes they'd
found in the attic.

It was here she had last seen her mother.

She climbed from the Jeep. The afternoon was bright
with sun, the insects humming in the humid heat, a typical Georgia day. The normality of it reassured her, and she
held on to that. There'd been little normalcy about her life
in the past weeks.

Her hand in Jake's, they climbed the wide steps that led
to the front door. It was unlocked, and they stepped into

the marble-floored foyer. The smells of home greeted her, and she breathed in a mixture of lemon-scented polish and flowers.

There were always fresh flowers at Belle Terre, a legacy of her mother. Today there were roses, pink and delicate, tucked into a Waterford vase, one of Madeline's favorites.

Dani let her gaze take in the foyer, the sweep of the staircase with its graceful banister that curved to the soaring second-story gallery, and tried to see it through Jake's eyes. Would he see beyond the trappings to the home beneath? Or would he be put off by the grandeur?

"You're here." Her father's booming voice, which he used to great effect in the Senate, welcomed them. "Come. Join us in the library."

With his shock of white hair and casual country clothes, he looked every inch the Southern gentleman he was.

Dani stood on tiptoes and kissed him. "Who's *us?*"

"I have a surprise for you. Victor's joining us for dinner tonight."

She nearly turned and ran, but good manners drilled into her by her mother from the time she could first say "please" and "thank you" required that she paste a smile on her face and, with Jake's hand at her waist, cross the foyer to the paneled doors leading to the library.

She had always loved this room, with its floor-to-ceiling bookcases, the march of books across the shelves, volumes that had clearly been read and reread. She knew of people who bought stacks of them just for effect. For her father, for herself, they were as necessary as breathing.

Victor rose from an oxblood leather chair and turned to face them, a smile of pleasure lighting his face. "Dani. It's good to see you again." He paused, his gaze raking Jake's imposing figure. "And, of course, your watchdog."

Dani bit down on her lower lip to curb the words that threatened to spill over. "Jake is hardly a watchdog," she said mildly. "He's a decorated soldier. We all have reason to be grateful to him. Me, most of all."

Victor assumed a chastened look. "You're right. Please forgive any slight. It was unintended, I assure you."

From beneath her lashes, Dani stole a look at Jake. She knew, just as he did, that Victor had meant the not-so-subtle insult. Only the tightening of Jake's lips, though, gave any indication of his reaction to the snub.

Her father seemed oblivious to the undercurrents and guided Jake to the gun collection that he kept housed in a glass case. "Finest collection in the state, if I do say so myself."

The senator's collection included muskets from the Revolutionary War era to dueling pistols of the early nineteenth century to more modern weaponry of the last century. Each gun was clearly identified with a small brass plaque, including a brief history of its origins.

"You have a fine collection, sir. You have every right to be proud."

Stewart Barclay's expression grew expansive. "Thank you. Dani has never been interested in it, but I enjoy showing it off to a man like yourself."

Automatically, Dani assumed the duties of hostess but couldn't help comparing herself to her mother.

Madeline Barclay was a true Southern lady, beautiful and gracious in a way Dani would never be. She had presided at Belle Terre with a gentle but firm hand, her dinner parties legendary, as was her devotion to her family.

The evening passed with only the occasional jab directed at Jake from Victor. In a moment alone with her father, while the other two men admired the gun collection, Dani asked, "Why did you invite Victor tonight?"

Her father frowned, his expression thoughtful. "I'm not sure that I did invite him. He called the other day, said how it had been too long since we'd seen each other. One thing led to another, and by the time we'd hung up, I guess I did issue an invitation of sorts. What's wrong? I thought you and Victor were friends."

"We were. Are," she corrected. "But he can be a little… intense sometimes."

Her father patted her back. "He means well."

"I suppose so."

The frown in her parent's eyes deepened. "There was a time when I thought you and Victor might make a match of it."

Dani didn't want to go there, so she changed the subject. "We've been following up on how Newton learned of my allergy to peanuts."

"Rabb's a good man. He proved himself the other night, saving you from that woman." Her father's voice turned grim. "I wish I'd been there. I should have been there. I should have never left town in the first place."

"You had a meeting in Washington," Dani reminded him gently. "I don't want or expect you to put your life on hold because some crazy person has me in his sights. That means he wins, and I won't let him."

"Thank you, my dear. You're more generous than I deserve." Her father coughed into his hand, a sign that he was embarrassed. "I shouldn't have been so high-handed, hiring Rabb without asking you. I was wrong."

That cost him, she knew, and she kissed his cheek. "I owe you an apology, as well. You hired Jake even when I didn't want you to. He saved my life."

"When I think of that woman trying to poison you, I want to take a horse whip to her."

"Me, too," Dani confided.

The shrewd gaze that had skewered many a political opponent was now aimed on her. "This Rabb. Is he important to you? More than just being your bodyguard?"

"We're friends." That much was true, at least.

This time his cough was a harrumph. "You'll tell me when you're ready. You're like your mama in that way. She kept things inside until she had them sorted out for herself." A whiff of sadness colored his voice, and then he held out his arm. "Let's get back to the others. I don't want Rabb to take Victor's head off. Not that he couldn't do it without breaking a sweat."

"You noticed that, too, did you?"

"I'm old, honey. Not senile. Of course I saw what was going on. Rather like putting a pet lamb in the same pen with a lion. Jake could take Victor down with a swipe of one paw."

He was right. That Jake treated the other man with for-bearance gave testament to his self-control. He reminded her of a predator trying to decide if it were worth the physical exertion to pounce on an irksome prey.

She put her hand on her father's arm and rejoined the other two men.

Here, in the dining room where her mother had presided over countless dinner parties, where old china and family silver were set with formal precision, Dani looked at the man she had at one time believed she would marry.

Victor was handsome in an Ashley Wilkes kind of way. Like the *Gone with the Wind* character, his patrician good looks were undeniably appealing, but he was deficient in something. Or, she reflected, perhaps it was only in comparison with Jake that he appeared to be lacking.

Of course, any man would come up short when compared to Jake Rabb. The thought startled her. Where had that come from? With his rough-hewn features and unruly hair, Jake was not conventionally handsome. But there was a quality to him that went beyond mere physical handsome-ness and made a woman, any woman, fully aware of herself, her femininity. He could be both gentle and harsh, depending upon the situation. The dichotomy was a powerful one.

Victor fit in the richly appointed room in a way that Jake never would. Yet Jake held his own with his quiet but insightful conversation and parried thrusts with the other man with a wit that clearly surprised Victor.

With her new recognition of Victor's pettiness and ego, she wondered what she had ever seen in him. True, he had been solicitous and supportive after her mother's disappearance, but that wasn't the basis for marriage. Marriage meant total commitment, an awareness of each other's needs, an acceptance of both the good and the bad. Victor would never have been able to give her what she needed, could never have accepted her for who she was.

She'd had a narrow escape back then. Her resolve to keep him at arm's length from now on was only strengthened by tonight's dinner.

In spite of his presence, she enjoyed herself, enjoyed the newfound harmony between herself and her father. She was coming to understand him in new ways and hoped he felt the same.

At the close of the evening, Victor took her hand, brought it to his lips. "Always a pleasure to see you, Dani. I realize I came across as heavy-handed at our lunch. I apologize for it and hope you won't hold it against me."

"Of course not." She withdrew her hand as quickly as possible and pretended not to notice the displeasure that flashed in his eyes. She turned her attention to her father. "Thank you, Daddy."

Jake held out his hand. "Thank you, sir."

The senator clasped his hand. "Thank you for keeping my daughter safe."

Outside, the afternoon had faded to the soft light of spring dusk. In the Jeep, Dani placed a hand on Jake's arm. "I know that wasn't how you'd planned to spend the evening, with Victor there."

"He doesn't bother me."

They made the drive back to the city in near silence, each wrapped up in their own thoughts. Millions of stars crammed the Georgia night, their brilliance in full view without the competition of the city lights.

Dani momentarily forgot that someone was after her, that her life was in danger until someone was caught. All she could think of was sharing the beautiful night with Jake.

She glanced at him, studying his profile. There was strength in the hard lines of his face, a strength tempered by compassion. Her feelings for him were more than a little confused, perhaps because she didn't know her own heart.

Could the heart be trusted? Or was it a traitorous vessel waiting to lead the unwary astray? Once before, she'd had feelings for a man, and that had ended badly. She'd hurt Victor and, in doing so, hurt herself, as well. She wouldn't—couldn't—make the same mistake again.

Jake had told Dani the truth. Victor Wingate didn't bother him with his little digs, his sly comments crafted as insults. He'd met men like him before, desperate to prove their power and resorting to putting others down to do so. However, Jake didn't trust the man. Wingate was clearly trying to ingratiate himself with the senator.

It didn't have to have anything to do with Dani. Wingate was ambitious, a lawyer on his way up. It was natural that he might turn to a powerful man like the senator for a leg up.

Why, then, did Jake have that itching at the back of his neck? In the battlefield, he'd learned to pay attention to that feeling. It had saved him and his men from walking into a trap more than once.

Beside him, Dani stretched. "I shouldn't have had that last piece of dessert."

"You could eat a dozen desserts and still not weigh more than a buck five."

She slanted a grin at him, her small white teeth gleaming in the darkness. "I'll have you know that I weigh considerably more than a hundred and five pounds."

"How much more?" he challenged.

"At least ten pounds more."

"Ah. I'll have to watch my step, then. At a hundred and fifteen pounds, you're a force to be reckoned with."

She swatted his arm. "I've been practicing those moves you and Shelley showed me every chance I get."

"Good." His light mood had vanished. "You may need them someday."

"You still think I'm in danger, don't you?"

It was tempting to lie to her, to tell her that after more than a week with nothing from her stalker, that the man—or woman—responsible had grown bored with the game, but lying wasn't his style. Dani deserved the truth.

"Yes, I do."

"I was hoping you'd lie to me," she said, voice so quiet that he had to strain to hear the words. "I wanted to believe it was all over."

"I know." He reached for her hand, squeezed it. "I wish I believed that." He changed gears. "When did your mother go missing?"

"April. Four years ago this month."

"What was your first instinct when she didn't come home?"

"I thought she was still angry with me. We'd had a fight that morning. She'd driven into the city to have breakfast with me. And we argued. It was pretty bad." She worried her bottom lip.

"What was it about?"

"Victor. Mama wanted me to break it off with him. She said she didn't think he was right for me. The more she told me what to do, the more determined I became to keep seeing him." A wry smile canted her lips. "Someone once told me that I could be stubborn."

Jake didn't return the smile. "He was right. What happened next?"

"Mama didn't return home that afternoon or that night. Daddy called me, asked if I knew where she was. I thought maybe she'd spent the day shopping, then taken a room in a hotel because it had gotten too late to drive home."

"Did she do that often? Spend the day in the city, then spend the night there."

"Mama was a firm believer in the power of retail therapy. She could shop me into the ground."

"When did you start to get worried?"

"The next morning. When neither Daddy nor I had heard from her, we knew something was wrong. Even when she was mad as a wet hen at either of us, she would never have let us worry like that.

"Daddy started calling her friends, her sister. No one had heard a thing. We couldn't file a missing-persons report until the next day, but we started checking with hotels, then hospitals. There was no record of her checking in."

"With your contacts and your father's pull, you must have called in some help."

"We did. I called in every favor I could think of. The police were on it. But there wasn't a trace of her. By the time Dad hired the private investigators, the trail, if there'd ever been one, had grown cold."

"You must have been frantic."

"I was. I could barely function and finally took a leave of absence from work. Everyone was very understanding.

"Eventually, I had to return to work and Dad got on with his life. For a long time, we were just going through the motions. After a while, things got better." Her small shrug was eloquent. "We kept living because we didn't have a choice."

"You're right," he said and thought of his own despair at

the deaths of his men. Wasn't that what he'd done? Forced himself to go on, even when he didn't see the point of anything? "You keep living because you don't have a choice."

"Is that what you did?"

Her perception didn't surprise him. "I tried holing up on my boat and shutting out the world. It was Shelley who pulled me out."

"By starting the business."

"Yeah. She saved my life."

"That's how I felt about Victor. He saved me. He can be pompous and rigid and a total jerk sometimes, but he was there for me. I can't forget that."

And Wingate played upon that, Jake thought. He used it to his advantage, cozying up to Dani when she was vulnerable, like now. Fortunately, she had come to her senses about the man.

"Why are you asking about my mother? Her disappearance can't have anything to do with what's happening now."

Jake wasn't so certain. Whoever was stalking Dani had intimate knowledge of her life, her family, her work. It wasn't too much of a stretch to put Madeline Barclay's disappearance and the stalking together.

"I'm just trying to make some pieces fit." He realized his answer wasn't really an answer at all. He'd hoped she'd leave it there. But Dani, being Dani, couldn't leave it alone, and he hadn't really expected her to.

"Mama went missing years ago. There's nothing to connect that with what's happening now." She took a deep breath. "It's over. Can we please not talk about it anymore?" As if to emphasize that, she said, "I need to pick up some more clothes. Can we stop at my apartment?"

Thoughtful, Jake pulled off the main highway onto the city street that would take him to Dani's apartment building. As he approached the parking garage, he slowed.

Maybe he was reaching at straws. All he knew was that

patterns tended to repeat themselves. Sometimes with a variation, but the pattern remained.

He pulled into a parking slot, helped Dani from the Jeep and hurried her into the elevator located nearby. Parking garages were a good place for attack. There was no sign of a threat; however, Jake didn't relax his vigilance.

Dani waited while Jake unlocked the door to her apartment, then drew his gun in preparation for checking the interior.

His harsh intake of breath told her something bad had happened. She moved to go inside but froze at his sharp "Stay put."

After long minutes had passed, he called, "Come on in. But watch your step." His face turned grim. "I'm calling Monroe."

Broken glass, overturned furniture and ripped upholstery greeted her. Dani knew enough to wait for the crime-scene techs before touching anything. Every piece of furniture was defaced in some way. She couldn't help her cry of distress.

Blood rushed to her head. Her sense of violation was so acute that she struggled to breathe. She bent from the waist, braced her hands on her knees. She started to shake.

Jake got the inhaler from her purse and was at her side in an instant. He put it to her mouth. "Breathe."

She took several lifesaving breaths, then set the inhaler aside. "I'm all right." It was a lie, and they both knew it.

He pulled her to him, sheltered her against his chest. "It's worse in your bedroom," he said quietly, and she knew he was trying to prepare her.

But nothing could prepare her for the destruction she found. She blinked against the scene before her, as though she could wipe it away, but the room came into sudden, shocking focus.

Her clothes had been pulled from the closet, slashed

into pieces. Perfumes and creams were spilled onto the floor and dresser. Drawers had been upended, their contents splashed across the ground.

The bed had been stripped of its spread, the mattress stabbed in dozens of places, stuffing strewn about in tufts of foam. The entire scene was one of such destruction that she felt as though she were on the job, viewing pictures of a crime.

A lone pillow sat atop the bed, a knife plunged hilt-deep into it, spearing a piece of paper. On it was written "You'll pay." The crudely printed message was all the more sinister for it appeared to have been written in blood.

Instinctively, she recoiled.

Jake pulled her away from the bed, but she couldn't tear her gaze from the hideous scarlet words scrawled on the paper. He framed her face with his hands, his touch gentle, but she could feel the tension in every finger.

When he dropped his hands, she felt the coldness seep back into her.

She tried to concentrate on the practical. "The knife looks like one from my kitchen set." She had seen countless crime photos. It came with the job. It was different, though, when the crime scene was your own home.

Is that what I'm supposed to learn from this, Lord? she asked silently. *Am I supposed to learn more compassion for the victims, more empathy?* It was a question she would have to take out at a later time and ponder.

She sniffed. There was something in the air…the scent of aggression, hatred? The air was foul with the stuff. Or was she being fanciful? She didn't know.

Jake placed a hand at the small of her back. She leaned into it, once more grateful for his quiet support. It was the only thing that kept her from spinning out of control.

At her feet lay scraps of paper. Kneeling, she started to pick them up before stopping herself. They were pieces of a photograph, one of her mother and herself together at Dani's graduation from law school. It had been a joyous day, filled with promise and expectation and heady excitement.

She dropped the scraps and stood. Her gaze moved around the room and landed on her collection of antique perfume bottles. They had once paraded across a shelf in bright array. They had been smashed against the wall, their jewel-like colors now shards against the hardwood floor. Unable to help herself, she picked up a broken piece.

The razor-sharp edge of the glass pricked her finger. Beads of blood appeared, but she scarcely registered that she was bleeding, so stunned was she by the hatred that must have spawned this destruction. Once more, she wondered what she could have done to cause this.

Jake took the piece from her and brought her finger to his mouth, where he gently kissed the blood away. "I'm sorry."

"They're just things." She tried to make herself believe it.

"But they were important to you. We'll find who did this," Jake said. "That's a promise, and I'm not in the habit of breaking promises."

Because he expected it, she nodded, but her gaze kept straying to the shards of glass that littered the floor. She had collected each bottle piece by piece, finding them at estate sales, in out-of-the-way antiques shops, even online.

He was trying to reassure her. She appreciated that, even as she wondered if she had the strength to fight this latest war, despite her resolve. She was shaking, more than she had before, and hated revealing that sign of weakness. She was a professional. Why couldn't she act like one?

"Give yourself time," Jake said, effortlessly reading her thoughts.

She was cold and still couldn't stop shaking. Her heart was thumping faster than it should have been, and she fought to get it under control. She had to get ahold of herself. This wasn't who she was. She was Danielle Barclay, Deputy District Attorney. She had stuck out a job no one thought she would get in the first place.

Stop shaking.

Jake took her hand, pressing much-needed warmth back into her cold fingers. The words *You will pay* were scrawled across her bathroom mirror in her favorite peach lipstick. Makeup had been spilled over the bathroom counter, along with shampoo and conditioner. The liquids had congealed into a nasty mess that was not mitigated by the scent of her shampoo. The flowery smell lent a macabre air to the scene.

"Why?" she asked brokenly. "Why?" She wrapped her arms around herself, but it was not enough to still the tremors that racked her body.

"Someone just upped the stakes." Jake's voice was hard, unforgiving, and she shivered at the barely controlled anger in it. He was in warrior mode now, his body tensed, poised for action, his face set in hard, resolute lines.

And now it was her turn. She knew Jake's anger was for her. She placed a hand on his arm, whether to calm him or herself, she wasn't at all sure.

God was with her. The feeling settled in her mind with quiet insistence. She grabbed on to it as she would a lifeline. Remembering the Lord was at her side, she let her practical nature take over, and with it came a blessed numbness that she welcomed, for it gave her the strength to act.

She couldn't start setting things to rights, not yet, though she longed to do just that. "I have to call the police. The insurance agent."

And then she found it, a small porcelain plaque, now broken, that had borne the words *The most important things in life aren't things.* No, she agreed silently, they weren't. Things could be replaced.

She squared her shoulders and prepared to do battle. Her gaze returned to the plaque, and she lifted her chin.

She refused to shatter over broken glass. She was made of stronger stuff than that.

Detective Monroe arrived within minutes. He gave a low whistle. "Somebody sure did a number on your place."

He and Jake went through the rooms. She didn't expect them to find any evidence as to who had trashed her apartment. There was just mindless destruction, as though whoever had done it wanted her to know just how much she was despised.

"This one wasn't Newton," Monroe said unnecessarily.

"No," Jake said thoughtfully, rubbing at his chin. "There's a kind of viciousness to it. The kind that a man who beats his wife might think up."

Monroe tugged at his beard. "You're thinking Brooks."

"I think it's worth checking his whereabouts for tonight, see if he has an alibi."

"He wears an ankle monitor," Dani reminded him.

"If a person's determined enough, there are ways around that. Just like he got around the lock. You didn't miss that it was unbroken, did you?"

Monroe shook his head. "No. I didn't miss that. And Brooks has himself a whole lot of hate for you, Dani, if you'll pardon my saying so."

If she hadn't been so weary and discouraged, she would have smiled. Detective Monroe was a Southern gentleman bred and born. Even in the midst of disaster, his breeding and manners shone through.

With the detective following them, Jake drove to his home. "Let me know what you find out about Brooks."

"Will do."

"Appreciate it." Jake took the plastic bag from Dani, draped an arm around her shoulders. "Let's see if we can get some sleep for what's left of the night."

She knew there'd be little sleep for either of them. The

viciousness of the attack was beyond anything she had witnessed. Was Jake right and Brooks was behind it?

She wouldn't put it past the man who had beat his wife until she was black-and-blue with bruises. If he thought this would scare her off, he was wrong.

Dead wrong.

When Jake heard Dani moving around in her room, he pushed himself up from the sofa and waited. He hadn't bothered going to his room. He was too wired.

He'd hoped Dani could get some sleep, but evidently she was as restless as he was. Who could blame her?

Her apartment had just been vandalized, her belongings slashed and destroyed. She'd been too shell-shocked to take it all in, which was probably a blessing. She needed to talk about it, to process what had happened. So he waited in the dark.

When the door to the bedroom opened, he was ready.

Only he wasn't ready for the pale-faced woman who stumbled into his arms. Automatically, his arms went around her and he held her, just held her. That was all. They stood there, locked in the embrace, for a long moment.

"I couldn't sleep," she said unnecessarily. "I tried."

"I know." There was more, so much more, he wanted to say, but he kept it to himself.

He reminded himself that she didn't need him to go all mushy on her right now. She needed his strength, and that was what he would give her.

"I can't stop thinking about it, but I want to. I want to put it out of my mind. At least for a little while." The corners of her lips quivered, then firmed, as though she wanted to cry, needed to cry, but was determined not to.

Still, there was a flash of brightness in her eyes, tears that, with a few blinks, were quickly banked.

Gently, he pushed her down onto the sofa. She was as unsubstantial as a wraith, as compliant as a child. She looked fragile, almost breakable at the moment. Her dark green eyes pleaded with him to talk about anything, anything at all, just so she didn't have to think about the destruction and the reality of what awaited her in the morning.

He'd never been any good at talking just to talk, but he'd give it a try, if it would take her mind, if only for a moment, from the nightmare they'd found at her apartment.

So he started talking. He talked about what it had taken to become part of Delta Force. Of the bone-numbing nights he'd spent on maneuvers. Of the sloshing through murky waters filled with creatures who made their homes there. Of the thrill of jumping into nothingness from the belly of a plane and then floating in a cloud-filled sky. Of the quiet before an air strike. Of the horror of watching friends die.

And, as he talked, he discovered something. He was talking as he'd never done with another living being. Certainly he'd never talked with the army shrink this way. Not even with Shelley had he shared this much.

He'd started talking about his Delta experiences to take Dani's mind off the devastation they'd found in her apartment. Now he was talking about things he'd shut away, and once he'd started, he couldn't stop.

After he'd emptied his soul of more than he knew was there, Dani looked at him with gratitude in her eyes. "Thank you."

His shrug was more than a little embarrassed. "For what? Bending your ear about things you didn't need to hear. Probably didn't want to hear."

"For sharing that part of you with me. I know you were trying to distract me, but it was more. Much more."

"I've never told anyone some of this." He couldn't look at her as he said the words. What was he trying to hide? Weakness? Vulnerability?

"Maybe you needed to."

He nodded. "Maybe I needed to."

"You love the army. I hear it in your voice. But you walked away."

"I couldn't stay. After what happened, I couldn't trust myself anymore. I was damaged in ways that had nothing to do with my leg. That…" He grimaced. "…that could be fixed. With a lot of therapy. The rest, I don't know." He thought of what Dani had endured with the disappearance of her mother. "How did you survive not knowing what happened to your mother?"

"I almost didn't. There were days when I could barely drag myself out of bed. Then I did the hardest thing I've ever done."

"What's that?"

"I got to my knees and asked the Lord to take the pain from my heart. I quit pretending that I could do it on my own."

"And did He? Take the pain?"

"In a way. I started living again. I got up each morning and went to work. After a while, the pain didn't hurt so much."

"How did you keep believing?" He didn't understand it, and only now did he realize that he really wanted to. There'd been a time when he'd have gone to the Lord and laid his heart bare, just as Dani had, but that time was past.

"I remembered the Lord never said that we wouldn't go through trials in this life, but that He'd always be there for us. For me. He's never let me down."

With all his heart, Jake wished he felt the same, wished he had a fraction of the faith of which Dani spoke so eloquently. "You're a special kind of woman, Danielle Barclay."

Jake pulled her closer, so close that he could feel the soft beat of her heart. Abruptly, he set her from him. He couldn't afford to get involved with this woman. Though he respected her faith, he didn't share it. Not any longer.

"Don't give up on the Lord," she said, "because I know He hasn't given up on you."

He chucked her under the chin with the ridge of his knuckles. "What do you say we both try to get some sleep now? I have a feeling that it's going to be a long day come morning."

She stood. "You're right. And thanks to you, I think I can sleep." She pressed her lips to his cheek. "Thank you, Jake. You're a good man."

That wasn't the first time she'd uttered those words to him, and he longed to believe her. Longed to believe that he wasn't the damaged man who had holes inside his heart that he feared would never be filled.

He walked her back to the bedroom, then closed the door gently behind her. Her words seeped into him, and, for the first time in a long time, he didn't feel the loneliness press into his heart.

EIGHT

When Dani came to work the following morning, it was to find her coworkers huddled together, whispering excitedly. They broke off when they saw her, but not before shooting guilty looks her way. It didn't take much guesswork to know they were talking about her.

Though she didn't socialize with Trevor and Sarah, she'd always thought she had a good working relationship with them, but now she wondered. It wasn't possible, was it? That one or both of them was behind the stalking? She gave a brisk nod and continued on her way.

An officer from the Atlanta P.D. was standing guard outside her office, his presence a grim reminder of last night.

Dani settled behind her desk and began going through her messages and emails when Clariss appeared, her face flushed. "Ms. Barclay—I mean Dani, would it be all right if I left a little early this evening? I have a date with my boyfriend."

Dani looked up from her keyboard and smiled. "Of course. Have a good time." She was glad Clariss had a date, a reminder that life went on. It was nice to think of something other than her own troubles.

Jake showed up after lunch. The morning had been filled with meetings with the insurance agent and claims adjuster. In between meetings, she'd sprinted through a store, picking up a few essentials with Jake at her side. Sometime, she'd have to carve out time to replenish her wardrobe.

When she'd finally made it to the office, Jake announced that he wanted to check with Monroe about lab results. She wanted to go with him but couldn't afford to take any more time from her own work.

The D.A.'s office didn't shut down just because her apartment had been vandalized. Her head pounded as she struggled to keep all the balls in the air without dropping one.

A key witness had backed out of testifying and was ready to bolt, and she was needed to put out the fire. She'd held his hand, promising him protection and then making good on that promise with a call to the Atlanta P.D. to arrange round-the-clock security, which made her feel guilty about the man stationed outside her office. The department didn't have enough manpower to assign someone to babysit her.

Last night, Jake had given her strength and truth, not pity or lies. Fear could be paralyzing. Jake understood that and had gotten her past it, had helped her to temper it with action. She owed him for that.

Someday, they'd sort out what was happening between them. Someday.

All of that went through her mind as she asked, "Any news?"

"The lab checked out the writing on the paper. It was pig's blood."

It was a relief that the blood wasn't human, though it was hard to find anything positive about what had happened.

"No news about the paper itself. Run-of-the-mill bond. Monroe's taking a look at Brooks's monitoring records. So far, they're clean. But a monitor can be short-circuited."

"So you said. A person would have to have specialized knowledge to do that, wouldn't he?"

"Maybe. Or maybe he bribes someone to do it for him. Or to look the other way when the monitor registers that he's moved outside the prescribed area."

She had already thought of that for herself. The implications were something she didn't like to consider but couldn't afford to overlook. "You mean someone in the department." A fresh shiver of fear skated down her spine. Her heart pounded in counterpoint to her growing headache.

Jake's silence was answer enough.

"I assume Monroe is checking on the people in his division."

"You know the drill. If he finds anything suspicious, he has to call in IA. No cop wants to do that to fellow officers. So he's taking it slow."

She understood the seriousness of calling in Internal Affairs. "Most of the cops in IA aren't witch hunters. They're good cops dedicated to weeding out dirty ones." She paused. "You think it's Brooks. Does that mean you think he's behind everything?" She'd thought about that during the night, praying that Brooks was the one who had been stalking her. He'd be arrested, and that would put an end to the terror. Somehow, though, she didn't think Jake believed Brooks was the stalker.

"I don't know."

Her sigh came in a long gust. "I wish he were. Then it would be over."

Jake skimmed his palm down her cheek. Her heart pinched a little, and she tried not to make the gesture into something it wasn't. Offering comfort, which was what he'd done, wasn't love.

And since when had she started thinking of the L word in connection with Jake? Obviously, she was more tired than she'd believed. Otherwise, she would never have entertained the thought.

"You know what I need?" he asked. "A hot-fudge sundae with whipped cream, nuts and a cherry on top."

"No one needs a hot-fudge sundae."

"I beg to differ. Hot-fudge sundaes are a known remedy for any number of ailments."

"Including a trashed apartment?"

"Most definitely." He grabbed her hand. "Play hooky with me. I happen to know of an old-fashioned ice-cream parlor where they serve real ice cream—the hard-packed kind, not the stuff that comes out of a machine."

It was tempting. "I have work," she said and gestured to the witness statement in front of her.

"Ditch it."

"I can't ditch work."

"Didn't you ever ditch class in school?"

She shook her head.

"Then you're overdue for a lesson in the art of playing hooky."

In the end, she did exactly that. She left work, though not without filing the papers in the proper place, told Clariss she'd be out for a while, then left the office in the middle of the day with the sole intention of eating a hot-fudge sundae.

A half hour later, she was bellied up to an ancient gray Formica counter, balanced on a red vinyl stool, shoveling vanilla ice cream drizzled with hot fudge into her mouth. "It's the best thing I've ever tasted."

"Better than Baked Alaska?" he asked, naming the dessert they'd eaten at her father's house last night.

She slurped up another bite, tasted, sighed. "Better." Was it only last night that they'd returned to her apartment and found the devastation? It seemed that a half a lifetime had passed in that span of hours.

"Told you so." He smirked, drawing her attention to the hot fudge that rimmed his mouth. Unashamedly, he licked it away with his tongue.

"Thank you. I needed this."

"Isn't that what I told you? You can need a hot-fudge sundae." The banter dropped from his voice.

She put down her spoon. "What I really need are some new clothes."

He laid some bills on the counter, leaving a generous tip. "We can go shopping right now."

"I can't. I have to take a deposition in forty-five minutes. Besides, I can do my shopping online. Just point and click."

"Doesn't sound like much fun," he commented. "Shelley's always telling me that the best part of shopping is the deciding."

"It is. But it can take hours. Days, even. I don't have that."

His hand at her elbow, Jake guided her from the parlor. She was surprised at just how much she had enjoyed the outing, and for the first time she could remember, she didn't look forward to returning to work.

In the end, the deposition took two and a half hours rather than the scheduled one. Dani was tired and nearing cranky by the end of it. Still, she kept her professionalism and was rewarded with getting the testimony she wanted on the record.

Jake had remained in the waiting room, and she wondered if he was as tired and cranky as she felt. Probably so. Neither one of them had gotten much sleep last night. She thought of the apartment she had furnished with such enthusiasm and care. Now she wondered if she'd ever be able to return there again.

Jake relieved her of her laptop and briefcase. "You're done for the day."

It was more an order than a question, and she treated it as such. "I'm done," she agreed. "And done in."

"I have something to show you." He herded her out to his Jeep and drove the twelve blocks to her apartment building.

"I don't want to see it," she said and was ashamed of the admission. Some torn clothes and ripped upholstery shouldn't have the power to upset her. Shouldn't have. But they did.

"You have to face it sometime."

Mentally bracing herself, she walked into the apartment. And stared.

The ruined furniture and torn books were gone. In their place was a sofa in a quiet color, two comfortable-looking chairs and a new bookcase, the shelves waiting to be filled.

"How did you…?" She broke off what she'd been about to say, too stunned to continue.

"As you said, point and click. After I met with Monroe this morning, I did some shopping of my own. I called in some favors, had some buddies of mine pick the stuff up and deliver it."

She wandered into the kitchen to find the spilled food and broken china gone.

"I also hired a cleaning crew," he said in answer to the question in her eyes.

The bedroom was next. A soft green spread covered a new mattress and box spring. The ruined clothes were no more. She opened her closet and gasped when she saw three suits in the spring colors she favored. "How did you know my size?"

"I looked at one of your blouses, saw the size and pointed my mouse. If you don't like them, we can return them."

Tears clogged her throat. Jake had done all this. For her.

"No one's ever done anything like this for me. Ever. I don't know what to say." The sting of tears behind her eyelids threatened to spill over. Jake didn't need her waterworks. She knew enough about men to understand that they weren't comfortable with a woman's tears.

He grabbed her hand. "C'mon. We're going home."

Twenty minutes later, the doorbell rang and a large man who looked nothing like a pizza delivery boy stood there, holding a flat white box and a large bag.

Jake made the introductions. "Dani, this is Sal. Short

for Salvatore. I told you about him. He's going to be helping us out for a while. Sal, meet Deputy District Attorney Dani Barclay."

Sal stuck out a large paw, enfolded Dani's hand in it. "Pleased to meet you, Ms. Barclay."

"It's Dani. And the same goes. How did Jake rope you into delivering pizza?"

"He said he'd buy. I'd do just about anything for good old American pizza." Already at home, Sal carried the box in to the kitchen. He dug in the plastic bag and came up with paper plates, napkins and three cans of soda.

"Sal, you're a lifesaver," she said fervently.

"I aim to please."

"Sal's going to stay with you when I can't," Jake explained. "Don't worry. He's one of the good guys."

By the end of the evening, Dani felt as though she'd known Salvatore Santonni all her life. His laid-back manner and easy conversation were a balm to her weary soul. She learned that he'd served with Jake in the Sandbox.

"It's a downright shame what some polecat did to your place," Sal said. "If I catch him, I'll skin him alive."

"How is it that you have a name like Salvatore Santonni yet talk like a good ol' boy?" she asked.

"Blame it on my mama. She was a real Southern belle, supposed to marry a family friend from Ole Miss, but she fell in love with a foreign exchange student named Luigi Santonni. It upset her mama and daddy something fierce, but they came around eventually. The rest, as they say, is history."

She lost the battle with a smile and finally let it have its way. "Seems like that history turned out pretty good."

"Thank you, ma'am. You're a real lady. Just like Jakey here said."

Dani turned to Jake. "Jakey?"

Sal spread his hands and cast an innocent smile upon her. "He told me I wasn't to call him Preacher."

"Preacher?" she asked.

Jake tossed a look her way. "It's a long story."

"It ain't long," Sal said in contradiction. "We called him Preacher 'cause he was always reading the Good Book."

"The Bible?" She couldn't keep the surprise from her voice.

Jake glared at his friend. "I've been known to crack it open once in a while."

"Don't let him fool you," Sal said. "He was always spouting scripture verses at us. Some of them even stuck."

"You talk too much," Jake muttered. "Give it a rest." He aimed a dark look at his friend. "Where're you staying?"

"I got me a place not far from here. I'll be here first thing in the morning."

"I like your Sal," she said after the big man had taken himself off. "He's nice."

Jake coughed out a laugh. "Sal's the one you want standing beside you when trouble hits. I hope you don't mind my hiring him, but I need someone to watch you while I do some more digging."

"Into Jerry Brooks?"

"Him and whoever helped him bypass that monitor."

"Why are you so convinced it was Brooks who trashed my apartment?"

"Human nature. Brooks has got himself a lot of rage. When it gets bad, he starts hitting. Someone. Or something. He couldn't get to you because I've been with you 24/7. But he could get to your apartment."

"That's another thing. How'd he get in?"

"Let's have a talk with your doorman, Barry."

"You can't think Barry had something to do with this." She refused to believe it.

"Not knowingly. But the kid's so green that I expect him to be sprouting grass any moment. How do you feel about another trip to your old digs?"

"Fine." That was a lie, and they both knew it.

Returning to her apartment building was bittersweet.

Barry, fresh-faced and eager to please, looked up and smiled. "Hey, there, Ms. Barclay. Mr. Rabb. What can I do for you?"

"You know about the trouble at my place last night?" Dani began.

His smile fell away. "I sure do. The police questioned me, right sharplike. I told 'em I didn't let anyone have a key. I'd never do that, Ms. Barclay. You know that."

"Of course I do. But maybe you noticed something?"

He frowned. "No, ma'am. Just like I told that detective, I didn't see anything out of the ordinary."

At a loss, she looked at Jake.

"What about someone who called you away from your desk?" Jake asked. "You do get calls from tenants, don't you?"

"Yes, sir. But I don't leave my post. The manager is real clear about that." He paused. "There was that policeman who came by."

"Asking questions about last night?" Dani asked.

"No. It was earlier. He wanted to know if I'd had any problems with homeless people hanging around." Barry darted a quick look between Jake and Dani. "I feel sorry for people who've got nowhere to go. In the winter, I let them hang out in the lobby if no one's around. Please don't tell anyone."

"We won't," she assured him.

"This policeman," Jake cut in. "You ever see him before?"

"No, sir. He said he was new and wanted to get a feel for the neighborhood. I told him this was a real nice place, with good people. He thanked me, then went on his way."

"How long did you talk?"

"Two minutes. Maybe three."

Jake exchanged a look with Dani. She knew what he was thinking. The fake patrolman could have distracted Barry just long enough for someone to sneak past him.

"Thanks, Barry," Dani said and pressed a bill into his hand. "You've been a real help."

"But I didn't do anything."

"Oh, but you did."

On the ride back to Jake's place, Dani thought aloud. "Someone could have gotten past Barry. But what about the security camera?"

"A security camera would be child's play for someone who could take out an ankle monitor."

"You're right."

If they were right in their supposition about Brooks, he was even more clever and dangerous than she'd first believed. It was with a troubled mind that she turned in for the night.

Jake knew Dani was nearing the end of her rope. She'd been stalked, nearly poisoned, now had her apartment vandalized. She'd held up admirably, but she was fragile right now.

Bringing Sal on to help guard her had been a stroke of genius. As he'd told Dani, Sal was the man you wanted standing at your side when trouble hit. He was also the man you wanted guarding your back when you couldn't do it for yourself. Since leaving Delta, Sal had knocked around, trying his hand at various things, including bounty hunting. He carried a pair of Flex-Cuffs with him, along with other tools of his trade.

Years ago, Sal had saved Jake's life in a forgotten village in the Afghan mountains. Jake had returned the favor a couple of years later when they'd taken fire in the mountains of Kazakhstan. They both bore the scars of those ordeals, inside and out.

Sal had been given the nickname Gentle Giant in the unit. His size and wizardry with weaponry were intimidating, but he had a tenderness to him that made him a favorite of children, wherever the unit had happened to be sent.

It was common among the men to share candy with village children, most of whom had never tasted it. Sal had made it a point to round up anything he could for the kids, even writing home and asking his family to send candy and small toys, which he distributed with a generous hand.

With Sal making sure that Dani was safe, Jake could spend the following days concentrating on investigating. He knew Brooks must have committed the vandalism. Now he just had to prove it.

As he got ready for bed, he admitted that he was more than tired. A nearly sleepless night the night before had left him sluggish and—he feared—unable to respond immediately should there be a threat. That was another reason he'd wanted Sal on board.

There'd been a time, not too long ago, when he'd gotten by on little or no sleep for days on end. When he'd hiked over rough terrain carrying an eighty-pound backpack of essentials. When he'd swum through frigid water against the current and jogged in desert heat without once breaking stride.

Though he hated to admit it, his body wasn't in that kind of physical shape any longer. Years of physically pushing his body beyond the normal limits had taken their toll.

He could still take on nine men out of ten, but it was that tenth that worried him. For himself, he didn't care so much, but Dani was in his charge now. A warrior accustomed to taking care of others, he would never forgive himself if something happened to her on his watch.

His watch. What was the saying? Old soldiers never died; they just marched to a new drummer. And that was what he was. An old soldier who was struggling to do the duty that had always defined him.

Sometimes he couldn't remember when he hadn't been fighting to survive. There were the years in the projects, when he had taken on anyone foolish enough to bother his little sister, when they had both battled against the poverty that sucked people under like a bog of quicksand.

When Shelley had graduated from high school and won a scholarship to college, he'd enlisted. There, he'd fought to make his way in the regimented and often brutal environment of military life.

He'd excelled at every challenge thrown at him, especially hand-to-hand combat and small weaponry. When he'd been singled out for training in special ops, he'd known he'd found his place.

Jake knew he was competing against other soldiers, even against the elements as he and the others trained in the worst conditions nature could throw at them. But, most of all, he understood he was competing against himself, trying to beat his best record. The challenge of it satisfied something deep inside him.

In the service, he'd found something he had never before experienced: a sense of belonging. Belonging to something bigger than himself, something that really mattered.

The work had intensified, with specialized skills added to the regimen. SERE training had convinced him that he wanted to be part of Delta Force, where the baddest of the bad volunteered to take the fight to the enemy on their own ground using what they'd learned in Survival Evasion Resistance and Escape.

For twelve years, he'd done just that, having been deployed to every trouble spot on the planet.

He'd risen in the ranks until he'd commanded his own unit. He'd believed that he would serve his full twenty before leaving the military.

Until Libya. Until his unit had been betrayed, sacrificed at the altar of politics and greed.

With a conscious effort, Jake emptied his mind of the past. He wished he still believed, that he could once again take the comfort he had always found in prayer. At one time, he'd wondered how those who didn't have faith got through a day, much less a lifetime, without prayer. It had been his sustaining force, his anchor, in a world that too often seemed to have gone mad.

He shut off the memories of when prayer had been a regular part of his life. He'd leave the praying to Dani and depend on himself.

The rap on the door awoke him. Instantly alert, Jake reached for his pants, pulled them on and went to the door.

"Preacher. It's me." Sal's deep voice sounded through the door.

Jake undid the locks and opened the door. "I hope you brought coffee."

"Coffee and the fixings for breakfast."

Sal's appetite was legendary among their unit. He routinely ate six eggs and six slices of bacon every morning. That he wasn't three hundred and fifty pounds of lard was one of those mysteries of nature.

"I'm a growing boy, Preacher. You know that."

Jake looked at the man who topped his own six foot two inches by another three, outweighed him by at least fifty pounds, and grinned. "That you are."

"Let me get breakfast started and you can catch me up on the scumbags I need to look out for."

While Sal made himself at home in the kitchen, Jake filled him in on everything that had happened. He started with the letters and phone calls, ended with Newton's trying to poison Dani at the awards night.

Sal's eyes narrowed as he listened. "I'd like to get my

hands on whoever's scaring a nice little lady like Dani that way."

"You and me both. I'm going to do some digging today, see what I can find out about beating an ankle monitor."

"There was a day that we'd have just held up that scoundrel by his ankles and shaken the answers out of him," Sal said, clenching and unclenching his big hands.

Sal had the softest heart of anyone Jake knew, but he had little patience for those who hurt the innocents of the world. "I enlisted," Sal had said upon meeting Jake in SERE training, "because the world is full of bullies. I never liked bullies on the school playground. I still don't like them. Hooyah!"

Jake thought about that now. Brooks was a bully, just as Dani had said. Bullies, like tigers, didn't change their stripes.

The law wouldn't allow it, but Jake had given serious thought to having it out with Brooks on his own terms.

After Jake had gone over everything, for his own benefit as much as for Sal's, his friend said, "You don't think Brooks is behind it?"

Jake had asked himself the same thing. Maybe he was wrong about everything. Maybe Brooks was the original stalker and had escalated his efforts to vandalizing Dani's apartment, but Jake's gut told him differently.

"I think Brooks is too hotheaded to have the patience to plan the stalking. His style is to strike fast and then get out." He lowered his voice. "I'd like you to do some checking on Dani's coworkers. They don't seem overly upset about what's happening to her."

"You think one of them could be involved?"

"I think I can't afford to overlook anyone."

Dani appeared, dressed in one of the suits he'd given to her, looking more rested than she had and ready to face the day. Jake couldn't help a spurt of pleasure that she'd liked what he'd picked out. The soft peach color set off her hair and eyes.

One of the things he liked best about her was her total unawareness of her appeal. She wore little makeup, which, in his opinion, made her all the prettier. Her hair was still damp, curling about her face.

She sniffed. "Bacon and eggs? Who do I kiss?"

"That'd be me, ma'am," Sal said and leaned down so that she could kiss his cheek.

To her credit, Dani didn't miss a beat and laughed delightedly. Jake felt an unfamiliar twinge and was outraged a moment later when he identified it as jealousy.

Jealous? Of Sal? The man was one of Jake's best friends.

Sal raised a brow, nodded. "I hope you're hungry. I've cooked enough here for the whole unit."

"I'm hungry enough to eat everything you've got," said Dani.

Sal loaded her plate with stacks of whole-wheat toast, a mound of scrambled eggs and six strips of bacon, fried to perfection.

Dani's eyes widened. "I'll be as big as a barn if I eat all this."

"Begging your pardon, ma'am, but you could stand a few extra pounds, if you don't mind my saying so."

Dani favored him with one of her thousand-watt smiles. "Thank you. You're a sweetie."

It was then that Jake witnessed something he'd never thought he'd see—Salvatore Santonni blushed.

After Dani offered a prayer, they dug into the country-style breakfast. Dani ate with relish and managed to polish off most of the toast, all of the eggs and five strips of bacon. "Delicious," she pronounced.

"I'll cook for you every meal," Sal promised. "Put some meat on those scrawny bones."

"I think her bones are fine just as they are," Jake snapped.

Sal flashed a grin in Dani's direction. "Preacher always did get a little testy when he overate."

"Preacher," Jake said with deliberate emphasis, "can speak for himself. And I did not overeat."

Dani stood and began clearing the table. "I'll take care of these and then we can go."

Sal took the plates from her. "My mama taught me that a gentleman always cleans up after himself." He dispatched the dirty dishes in short order. "If you're ready, ma'am, we can be on our way."

"Let me grab my purse. And, Sal? It's Dani."

Jake tried to defuse Dani's insistence that she go with him to question the officer who oversaw Brooks's ankle monitor. "You have your own work to do," he pointed out.

Dani nodded. She was busy with her cases, most especially those of Newton and Brooks. That didn't mean, however, she didn't want to be part of the investigation.

She wondered about Jake's motives for not wanting her to accompany him to interrogate the officer.

Did he want to approach the officer man-to-man? She knew some men were put off by a woman's presence.

Jake's and her research into the policeman assigned to monitor Brooks revealed that Charles Washington had been divorced twice and had a reputation among his female co-workers of being difficult to get along with.

"I'm going with you," she said.

Looking none too happy, Jake only nodded.

They tracked the officer down, and she was immediately struck by the man's belligerent attitude.

"I've got a bunch of irons in the fire," Washington told them, sweating heavily even in the air-conditioned building. "I don't have time to tell you what you can see for yourself." He made a show of shuffling a pile of papers.

"We have just a few questions," Dani said, deliberately taking the lead. "First, how accurate is the monitor?"

Washington shifted his weight, and his overburdened chair creaked in protest. "It's state-of-the-art."

"What does it take to fake the results?" she persisted.

A heavy sigh of impatience. "I told you, the monitor is state-of-the-art. A hundred percent accurate."

"Can we look over your report?"

Washington shoved the paper in her direction.

With Jake looking over her shoulder, Dani scanned the report, failing to see any deviation in movements. Brooks went to work, returned home and repeated the pattern day after day. Two nights ago showed him at home.

"You can see Brooks is right where he was supposed to be," Washington said. "Including Monday night."

"How did you know we were interested in Monday night?" Jake asked.

Washington flushed. "I heard, okay? Nothing's secret round here."

Dani filed that away. "Mind if we make copies of this?"

Washington gestured to an ancient copy machine. "Have at it."

After making the copies they needed, Dani turned back to the man. "Thanks for your time."

More expansive now that his questioners were finished with him, Washington leaned back in his chair. "Brooks has kept his nose clean. No way he was outside the prescribed perimeter."

"Thanks again."

Interesting, Dani thought on her way to Jake's Jeep. Washington had gone out of his way to champion Brooks. It might pay to check into the officer's background, see what chains they could rattle.

Two hours later, Jake and Dani had what they wanted. Washington had big-time money problems. The man had two ex-wives, was behind over six months in alimony and child-support payments. He also liked expensive cars.

Now they had to find a tie between Brooks and Washington. That took more digging, but they found what they were looking for when they went back to the men's college days.

"College ties can run deep," Dani said.

Jake nodded, his face grim when they found the link. Both men had attended Georgia Tech. What was more, they had both played on the school's football team.

By four-thirty, Jake and Dani made their way back to the Atlanta P.D. They found Monroe holed up in his office.

"What do you have for me?" the officer asked.

Jake took the lead this time. "A connection between Brooks and the officer handling the monitor."

Monroe's eyes narrowed. "You're kidding."

"Both attended the same college at the same time. Both were on the football team. Washington played wide receiver to Brooks's quarterback."

"Don't get much closer than that." Football wasn't just a sport in the South. For many, it was a way of life.

Taking turns, Dani and Jake filled in Monroe on what they'd discovered about Washington's finances.

"He's hurting," the detective agreed. "No doubt about it."

"Any chance you can get a court order to look at his bank statements?" Dani asked.

"Audit trail," the detective said with a knowing nod.

She nodded. The cliché of "follow the money, find the truth" usually held true.

"I've got a couple of lines I can tug." Monroe checked his watch. "It's about quitting time over at the city offices. Do you need to be there?"

Jake looked at Dani. "I've arranged for a friend to stay with Dani, so, yeah, I want to be there."

"If he's one of yours, I figure he's solid."

Jake dipped his head at the implied compliment. "He is.

Sal will take down anyone who tries to get to her. And he won't be fussy at how he does it."

"That's good enough for me." Monroe steepled his fingers together. "Assuming Brooks managed to beat the ankle monitor and sneak past the doorman. How did he enter the apartment? CSU didn't find any evidence that the lock had been tampered with. It's like he just waltzed right in."

Dani had been pondering the same thing. It bothered her more than a bit.

"Dani told me she hadn't given out any keys to her place," Jake filled in. "Then there's the security code. Whoever did it needed to get past that, as well."

"Of course, if a person beat the monitor, chances are he wouldn't have a problem with getting past a security code."

"You're right."

The three of them kicked around other ideas. "Even if we prove Brooks did the vandalizing, you think we're still looking for someone else for the stalking," Monroe summed up.

"That's how it's shaking out for me," Jake said.

Though Dani had expected his words, she couldn't stifle her disappointment. It would have been over if they could prove Brooks was behind the stalking. She stiffened her resolve. She wouldn't let this defeat her.

"I'll get on Charles Washington's bank records," Monroe said, standing. "Keep me in the loop."

"Count on it." Jake took Dani's elbow and escorted her from the station.

"I expect you to do the same with me," she said once she and Jake were outside. "Keep me in the loop. It's my life on the line."

"Do you think I've forgotten?"

She took in the hard expression in his gaze. "No." Jake would protect her with his own life. She had no doubt of that. No doubt at all.

NINE

"A police officer altered the files? Are you sure?" Dani didn't want to believe what Jake had discovered.

She'd come across a few dirty cops in her years with the D.A.'s office, but they were the exception. Most of the men and women who wore blue were honest, hardworking and dedicated to the job. To have a police officer, perhaps even one she had worked with, directly try to sabotage her made her feel sick inside. It brought the whole thing of corruption right to her own front door.

"Monroe is checking out Washington's financial records, but, yeah, we're pretty sure. He and Brooks went to school together, even played on the football team at the same time. Brooks had motive, means and, with Washington in his pocket, the opportunity."

Sal had been silent up until then. "You think I should have a talk with this Brooks fellow, Preacher?"

Despite her heartsickness, Dani smiled. Sal, the Gentle Giant, had been at her side every minute of the day. He had made sure she'd eaten lunch, even going so far as to order a bistro sandwich from her favorite delivery place.

He'd stared down anyone who tried to approach her and had, she'd learned from Clariss, once intimidated even the great man himself, Leonard Freeman. He was well-read and could discuss anything from Dante's *Inferno* to the latest vampire series.

Dani answered for Jake. "No, Sal. I think we can leave him for the cops. The honest cops, that is," she amended.

"Monroe's bringing Brooks in tonight. Tomorrow, we'll have a little question-and-answer session with him."

Dani couldn't help herself. She shivered. The hard look in Jake's eyes along with the grim tone of his voice didn't bode well for Brooks.

"What about Washington?"

"If Monroe finds what we think he will—payments from Brooks to Washington—he'll bring Washington in tomorrow, as well. IA will get their chance at him."

"I want to question him, too."

Sal rubbed his hands together. "I don't know about y'all, but all this talk of corruption has given me an appetite. Hooyah!"

Jake grinned. "When *aren't* you hungry?"

Sal scratched his head. "Don't rightly remember."

Dani smiled. "You're a fraud. I heard you discuss Elizabethan poetry with Trevor Ryan at the office. That good-ol'-boy act of yours won't cut it."

Sal nodded. "You got me there, ma'am. But I do it so darn well, don't I?"

"You do at that."

They decided to go out for Thai. "The spicier the better," Sal said. He picked Dani up, swung her around. "We're going to fatten you up yet."

Though she wished it were Jake picking her up, she laughed up at Sal. "If you have your way, the whole world will fatten up."

With the two men flanking her, they made the short trip to the elevator, took it down to the building's parking garage. Sal, weapon raised, walked ahead of Jake and Dani, peering into the shifting shadows cast by the overhead lights.

When Dani slanted a glance at Jake, he said only, "Sal's the best at scouting out Tangos."

She supposed that Sal's skill for spotting enemies ought to make her feel safer. Instead, it only emphasized the seriousness of the situation. "Why can't you believe it's Brooks?"

Jake didn't answer at first. "I've learned not to ignore my gut," he said at last.

"Your gut? What does your gut have to do with anything?"

"It saved my hide and the lives of my men more than once." In the garish lights of the garage, she saw the shadow pass over his face and guessed he was remembering the time his gut hadn't saved his men.

Silently, Dani took his hand, gave it a hard squeeze.

The look that passed between them told her that Jake knew what she was doing and why.

When they reached the Jeep, Sal had already opened it, checked the interior. "Everything's clean, Preach."

Jake nodded his thanks. He helped Dani inside, closed the door behind her and jerked his head to the backseat.

Sal grimaced. "How am I going to get all of me in that teeny, tiny space?"

"I can take the back," Dani offered.

Jake gave an offhand shrug. "Sal's fit himself into tighter spots than the back of a Jeep."

"He's right." Sal folded himself into the backseat, then leaned forward and wrapped a beefy arm around Jake and Dani each. "Where're we going, Mom and Dad?"

"Put your seat belt on and be quiet."

Their byplay was easy and friendly, Dani reflected. Apparently serving in the same unit together had made for an easy camaraderie that carried beyond the time serving their country.

She was discovering that she liked Jake's friend. Without thinking, she said just that. "I like you, Sal Santonni."

"That makes us even, ma'am, 'cause I like you right back."

"You're sweet."

"I'm going to remember that," Jake put in. "Sal Santonni being called *sweet*. I think I'll let the rest of the men know. They'll thank me."

Despite his light words, Dani couldn't help but notice the displeased look in Jake's eyes. Had she done something to make him angry?

"Preach, you wouldn't really do that, would you?" Horror heightened Sal's voice to a squeak.

Dani caught a glimpse of Sal's face in the rearview mirror. Mortification filled it. "I'm sorry."

"Not your fault, ma'am. It's Preacher. For all his Bible spouting, he can be a hard man. Real hard. He made us toe the line something fierce over there in the Sandbox."

"I think it's like your good-ol'-boy routine. That hard exterior is just an act."

Sal winked at her in the mirror. "I think you could be right about that."

The restaurant was busy with the late work crowd. With his hand at the small of her back, Jake asked for a booth to the rear of the dining room. After seating her, he then made sure that he took the seat with his back to the wall. Dani had noticed he'd done the same thing in other places.

Sal caught her look and explained, "Back to the wall is instinctive to a soldier. Or a cop."

It must be hard, she reflected, to always be on duty, to never be able to relax. Her gaze rested on Jake and she warmed at what she saw there. Was there more in his eyes than feeling protective of a client? She wanted to think so.

When the waitress appeared to take their orders, she sized up the table's occupants and turned to Jake. He gave their orders to the twentysomething woman, who favored each of the men with an especially warm smile. She all but ignored Dani, who watched with a big smirk at her two escorts.

"You've got an admirer," she said, including both men in her smile.

"She's too old for me," Sal said promptly. "I'm just a babe in the woods compared to a big-city gal like that."

Jake grumbled something undecipherable.

What was wrong with him? Dani wondered. He'd been in a strange mood all evening, even growling at his friend. "Is something wrong?"

"Nothing you can help with," he muttered.

Sal, however, didn't seem upset. If anything, he appeared amused.

The big-city gal in question returned with their orders, once again directing big smiles in Jake and Sal's direction. Jake, Sal and Dani dug in, sharing dishes, sampling from each other's plates.

For that hour, Dani's troubles fell away, the worry that had been so much a part of her faded, and she was simply a woman enjoying dinner with two attractive men.

Not a bad way to end the day. Not bad at all.

He should have been pleased that Dani and Sal got along so well, Jake thought. He should have. But he wasn't. The whole jealousy thing was new to him. He'd never had a problem with jealousy before.

What was going on with him anyway? This wasn't like him. Nothing he'd done or felt in the past couple of weeks was like him, not since he'd first laid eyes on Dani.

The acknowledgment did little to soothe his temper, and he was in a foul mood by the time they returned to the house.

He dropped Sal off at his truck where he'd parked on the street.

"See you tomorrow, Dani," Sal called as he climbed out of the Jeep.

"Tomorrow," she echoed. Then she turned to Jake. "What

was that all about? We were having a nice dinner and all of a sudden you turn all Delta Force scary."

"I was Delta Force," he reminded her.

"But you were never scary. Not this way."

"I'm sorry." He couldn't tell her that he was jealous of his friend. Couldn't tell her that he had feelings for her way beyond those of a bodyguard for a client. That would be unprofessional at best, not to mention unethical. So he kept his feelings to himself.

She reached for his hand, squeezed it. That sweet, quiet gesture had his heart.

The urge to tell her about his feelings was overwhelming. Dani was everything he'd ever wanted. Smart. Compassionate. Beautiful. He'd never met a woman who lived her faith as Dani did. She brought it to her work, used it to make herself a better D.D.A. and, more, to make herself a better person.

She could no more separate herself from her faith than she could turn away a friend who needed her help. Both were part and parcel of her.

"You're a good man. You deserve to be happy."

"I don't know about that." That was the most he could say, that he wanted to be a good man. He knew he could do better than he did. Every day, he struggled with the need to forgive those who had cost the lives of his men.

Spending time with Dani, seeing her belief in action, had sparked a kernel of his own faith.

"The things I've seen, the things I've done…" He shook his head. "I don't deserve happiness."

"How can you say that?" Dani's voice turned urgent. "You do deserve to be happy. More than most."

He shook his head. "That might have been true once. Not after my last mission. I let down my men. I let down myself."

"That wasn't your fault. You did everything you could to save them."

"It wasn't enough."

She reached for his arm, wrapped her fingers around his wrist. "Happiness can be yours, Jake. But you have to want it."

He summoned a faint smile. "You almost make me believe that. You make me want the happily-ever-after ending in the books I used to read to Shelley."

"It's yours for the asking."

"You mean asking the Lord."

Her nod confirmed his words, but he wasn't buying it. Even with the Lord's help, he didn't know whether he could find it in him to let go of the anger and bitterness that filled his heart.

"You're some kind of lady, Dani Barclay."

"And you're some kind of man."

"Looks like we've got our own mutual admiration society going on," he said at last, needing to break the intimacy of the conversation.

Her smile told him that she understood what he was doing. And why. "I can't think of anyone I'd rather have in that society than you."

Jake put the Jeep in gear and drove through the dark streets to his home.

Dani was moved by Jake's words. And for the first time in a long time, she wanted more than simple friendship from a man. She wanted to get close to someone, to let him into her life, into her heart.

She was so tired of being alone.

In her heart, she'd been alone since her mother had left. Of course she loved her father and knew that he loved her, but he had closed off a part of himself with his wife's disappearance.

There had been Victor. He'd been there for her at the worst time of her life, and for that, she would always be grateful, but he had never touched her heart the way Jake did.

Jake had the air of a loner. She understood that, as, in many ways, she was also a loner. It was easier sometimes to be alone than to be surrounded by people and still be alone inside, where it counted.

With Jake, she no longer felt alone.

She stole a glance at him in the dark interior of the Jeep. His chiseled profile belied the tenderness he showed on rare occasion.

He turned to her, his face revealing a layer of emotion she hadn't seen before. "You're staring."

Caught, she could only nod.

"Why?"

"Because you're nice to look at." That much was true. Jake would never be termed *handsome,* but he had something more appealing than mere handsomeness. His appeal was that of an honorable man determined to do the right thing, whatever the cost to himself.

His personal code, she'd learned, was one of such innate integrity that she wondered if he was even aware of how rare that was these days. Did he take it for granted because it was so ingrained within him?

Thoughts swirled through her mind during the trip to his home. Jake had worked his way into her life, into her heart. If not for the stalking, they would probably have never met.

No!

Her heart rejected that notion.

Still, she couldn't deny the unusual circumstances of their relationship. Was that what prompted her feelings for him? The sense of safety she felt when she was with him? A misplaced sense of gratitude?

Once more, she rejected the explanation.

Please, God, she prayed, *let me find the strength to resist what I'm feeling.*

Her father had loved her mother with his whole being. When she'd disappeared, he'd suffered so intensely and fallen into such a deep despair that Dani had feared she'd lose him, as well.

No, love didn't always bring happiness. It was a lure for the unwary, rife with pain and misery. She'd be a fool to fall into that trap.

She stiffened her resolve. Jake was a good and honorable man, but he wasn't for her. Hadn't she already warned herself about mistaking gratitude for love? She felt safe with Jake. That was all.

TEN

"We've got a break." Monroe's voice came over the line, the usually slow-talking detective speaking rapidly, almost urgently.

"What is it?" Jake asked. He and Dani were still at his home, the only place where he felt confident she was safe.

"Newton apparently had a change of heart. Or, more likely, she started listening to her lawyer, who pointed out that she wasn't doing herself any good by not cooperating."

"What did she say?" Right now, Jake didn't care about Newton and her angling for a deal.

"You'll probably want to hear it yourself, but, basically, she said that she got an email with the information about Dani's peanut allergy, plus where she was going to be that night and how to get hired on by the caterer. Get this—the email contained a job application form. All Newton had to do was fill in the blanks, send it in." Monroe paused a beat. "You know what this means."

"Yeah." Jake's mind was already jumping two or three steps ahead. Whoever had sent Newton the email knew things about Dani, private things that weren't readily available to others. "It's nothing we didn't already suspect."

"But here's the thing—we've got the IP address of the email. Now it's just a matter of tracing it back to its source." An edge of excitement crested the detective's normally gravelly voice.

Jake wished he felt more hopeful about their success at

that. Anyone sophisticated enough to bypass the video at Dani's apartment probably knew how to cover his or her electronic tracks. He said as much to Monroe.

"I hear you. But it's something. More than we had."

"What about Washington's financial records?"

"We've got them, too. It's just like we thought. Two large deposits were made into Washington's checking account. We traced them back to Brooks. Who do you think will turn on the other first? Washington or Brooks?"

"It's a toss-up. They're both scum." And it was certain that neither of those men had anything to do with the email sent to Newton. The individual who had done that was savvy enough to know how to conceal his identity. Brooks and Washington were arrogant enough or stupid enough to not even try to hide the transaction.

Monroe growled. "You've got that right. If I had my way, I wouldn't deal with either of 'em, but if they've got information that'll lead us to the stalker, then I'm willing. This thing has gone on long enough."

Jake appreciated the detective's honesty as well as his dislike of working with either Brooks or Newton, but Monroe was right. "Sounds like you're thinking the same way I am. That Brooks was put up to this, just as Newton was. They're being used by someone who knows enough about Dani to know how to get to her."

"It plays for me. I figured it would for you, too. Our stalker knows enough about Dani to know who else has it in for her, whom he could manipulate. All he had to do was tap into those feelings. Revenge is a powerful motive."

"Something still bothers me," Jake said, thinking aloud. "What about the security system in Dani's apartment? Even if someone got by the doorman, he'd still have to deal with the security code."

"I don't know." Jake could hear the frown in the other

man's voice. "We just keep connecting the dots. Pretty soon, we'll have the whole picture."

"Yeah." But would they have it in time? Dani was running on empty. She had held up admirably for weeks, but how much more could she take? The shadows under her eyes grew deeper with every day.

"Thanks for the heads-up," Jake said. He heard Dani stirring. "If you find anything more…"

"Don't worry. I'll keep you in the loop."

When Sal showed up, he made a show of holding up his hands and backing away. "I came bearing gifts." He dropped the package he carried onto the kitchen table. The aroma of yeast and chocolate wafted from the white bakery bag.

"About last night…" Jake began.

"No problem." Sal grinned. "I get the picture. You like the lady. Can't say I blame you." His grin widened. "You've got good taste, buddy."

For all his teasing, Sal was a good friend, who said more with a look than most people could get out in a thousand words. "Thanks."

Sal nodded toward Dani's room. "She up?"

"I heard sounds. Should be a few more minutes before she comes out." Jake was beginning to know Dani's routine, knew she liked to take time with her morning prayers.

"Good. 'Cause I wanted to talk to you. Privatelike. When I was with Dani yesterday, I noticed things. That so-called colleague of hers, Sarah something-or-other? She's got it in for our girl."

"How so?"

"I saw her sidling up to the big man there, telling him how it is that Dani isn't pulling her own weight. She was all sugar and honey, saying it wasn't Dani's fault and all, that she'd take up any slack caused by 'Dani's inattention to work,' so he shouldn't worry." Sal made a disgusted sound.

"You think Sarah's involved in the stalking?"

"I wouldn't be surprised. I'd face an enemy soldier any day over a female like that one."

"You and me both." At least with the enemy, you knew what you were facing. A backstabbing colleague took the battle to a whole different level.

"Another thing. That A.D.A. He's not popular with the rest of the office. I got that from one of the secretaries."

"From Clariss?"

"Yeah. She tells me that Ryan would walk all over Dani if given half a chance. I caught him shooting her daggers when he thought no one was looking."

"I figured that out for myself. He's been passed over for the next-to-top spot several times and now Dani has it. She's not only younger and better liked—she does the job more effectively than he'll ever hope to. He doesn't strike me as someone who steps aside for anyone."

"Looks like we're on the same page," Sal said, fishing a doughnut out of the bag. "My great-grandmother would have called a whiner like that a pantywaist." He took a bite out of the doughnut and sighed in satisfaction. "Goes without saying that I'll be keeping a close eye on both those characters." He switched gears. "About that other matter."

"Dani's mother's disappearance?"

"Yeah. I did some searching on the stories about it. Four years ago, it was national news. All the major networks ran stories on it. A sitting United States senator's wife walks out, just disappears into thin air. There was never any talk about another man. And even if there was someone else in the picture, why would a classy lady like that just disappear, walk away from her daughter? Word was they were tight."

"That's what I get from Dani." Jake knew she still grieved over her mother.

"I did some checking on her from the week before she disappeared. She hadn't canceled any of her social engagements, and the woman had lots of those—charity stuff, lunches with friends, et cetera. One thing—she was supposed to go to a doctor's appointment downtown." Sal paused. "An oncologist."

"Cancer? Do you know what kind?"

Sal shrugged. "No. I checked with the doctor's office, explained I was working for the daughter, but got nowhere. You know how doctors are about privacy and stuff like that. The thing is, the appointment was scheduled on the same day the lady did her vanishing act."

"You're thinking maybe she was afraid of facing bad news and just took off."

"Maybe. But she'd still leave a trail. People always leave some kind of trail, especially civilians like that. They don't know how to cover their tracks. I went down all the usual roads, checked for credit-card activity, variations of her name, like if she's using her maiden name, even checked with an old girlfriend who works at the DMV.

"The bottom line is I came up with a big fat zero. I'm sorry."

"Not your fault. Dani's father hired the best P.I. firm in the South and they couldn't turn up anything either. It's like the lady just dropped off the face of the earth."

"I made a few calls, checked with the guy they put on it. He's a good man, has a reputation of getting the job done no matter what. He's still scratching his head over what happened to her." Sal's voice dropped. "He's of a mind that someone offed the woman and buried her somewhere she'd never be found."

"Did he share his suspicions with the senator?"

"No. There was no proof of foul play, so he couldn't see any upside in telling the family that he thought the wife and mother was dead."

Jake had thought the same thing. Someone like Madeline Barclay didn't just up and leave her family for no reason. "I owe you," he said seriously. "I owe you big."

"Hey, we're buddies. Buddies have each other's back. You saved my bacon over in the Sandbox."

"Seems like I remember it the other way around." Jake recalled Sal pulling him from a pile of rubble while they were taking heavy artillery fire.

"We did right by each other," Sal agreed. "You know any of the guys would lay it on the line for you. I'll keep your lady safe. You find out who this polecat is."

Jake clasped his friend's arm, a wordless gesture of thanks, and knew that words were unnecessary. Sal had come through for him, just as he always had.

When Dani appeared, both men were chowing down on chocolate-covered doughnuts.

"I hope you saved me one with sprinkles."

Jake grinned. Another thing he adored about Dani. She had an unquenchable sweet tooth and didn't mind indulging it. She'd never be one of those women who nibbled on a piece of lettuce and called it dinner.

Though Dani's eyes had a bruised appearance, she wore a smile that went straight to his heart.

He handed her a heavily sprinkled doughnut. "Saved this one especially for you."

"Thanks."

The warmth in the single word stopped him in his tracks, enough so that he had to think about what he said next. "I know the way to this girl's heart." He gestured to her, kept it light.

Finally, he was able to get his brain in focus. "Monroe found the financial connection between Brooks and Washington. Those two are going down, for conspiracy, bribery, breaking and entering and a bunch of other stuff."

Dani's eyes took on a determined light. "That's just what I was waiting for. Brooks will be put away for so long, he'll never have another chance to hurt his wife, Stephanie."

It was typical of Dani that she would think of another person before herself. He no longer wondered why she'd taken a job with the D.A.'s office when she could have made five or ten times what she was making by working in the private sector. Dani wanted to make a difference and saw her work as a way to do just that.

It shamed him that he'd ever thought her to be a pampered society princess. She worked at a job where she saw the worst that one man could do to another and still she retained a well of compassion and an unshakable belief in the Lord.

She polished off the doughnut, grabbed another one. "Let's get me to work. I can't wait to nail Brooks to the wall for this."

Sal whistled. "What a woman. Dani, sweetheart, will you marry me?"

She laughed and hugged his arm.

At Jake's glare over her head, Sal grinned unrepentantly.

Jake accompanied them to Sal's truck, gave Dani a hand up, then, impulsively, pressed a kiss to her cheek. "Stay safe," he whispered.

"I'll be fine." She gestured toward Sal. "He scares off anyone who even looks at me cross-eyed."

Sal gave a mock ferocious growl. "I aim to please, ma'am."

Jake shut the door behind Dani. "Keep her safe," he said to Sal over the hood of the truck.

"Nobody's going to hurt your lady as long as I'm on the job."

Jake pondered his friend's words. Dani wasn't his lady, but he cared about her more than he'd ever cared about another woman. Many a time he'd trusted Sal with his own life. Now he was entrusting him with something far more precious.

Dani was on fire. She had enough ammunition to put away Brooks until he was grizzled and gray. Her first order of business, though, was to call Stephanie.

Quickly, she filled in Stephanie on the latest with her soon-to-be ex-husband. "I can't believe he'd do that to you," Stephanie said. "He must be crazy."

"We think someone put him up to it," Dani explained. "But I'm guessing it didn't take much convincing for him to come after me."

"I'm just glad you weren't there when he trashed your apartment. If you had…" Stephanie's voice trembled "…he would have hurt you. Just like he did me."

Dani's heart went out to the other woman. At the same time, though, she knew she'd never have submitted to Brooks's brutality without a fight, and now, with the training Shelley and Jake had been giving her, she felt confident she could defend herself.

But she said none of that to Stephanie. As much as Dani tried, she could never fully put herself into the other woman's place. Stephanie had been humiliated and terrorized for so long by her husband that no one could blame her for failing to fight back.

"I just wanted to let you know that you won't have to worry about him. He's never going to be able to hurt you again."

Soft sobs came over the phone. "Th…thank you. You can't know what this means to me. I can finally have a life."

"You did the hard work," Dani reminded her. "You found the courage to testify against him. All I did was offer a little encouragement."

"You did a lot more than that." Stephanie's voice took

on strength. "I'm going back to school. I always did pretty well in my classes—that is, until I met Jerry and he convinced me that I didn't need to have a career. I'm going to get my RN. That's what I always wanted, to be a nurse."

"That's wonderful," Dani said sincerely. "You'll make a great nurse."

"I hope so. It'll be a chance to help others."

When Dani hung up, she gave a silent prayer of thanks that Stephanie had been given this second chance. *I know this came through You, Lord. You're in charge. You are always in charge.*

She looked up to find Sal watching her. She didn't explain why she was praying, nor did he ask her why, but the look he gave her was one of understanding and approval. She felt warmed all the way through.

"I got a message from Detective Monroe. He's had Brooks picked up and invited me to sit in on the interrogation."

Sal got to his feet. "Let's go. I can't wait to get a gander at this lowlife."

Trust Sal to not mince words.

Within fifteen minutes, they were seated in an interrogation room of the Atlanta P.D. Brooks, accompanied by his lawyer, was handcuffed and shackled to the floor by chains.

She felt a moment's pity for the man who had everything and then had chosen to throw it away. Then she recalled the battered picture Stephanie Brooks had made when she was brought into the hospital after the last beating. The woman deserved justice; more, she deserved a chance at life, a real life, not one controlled by a sadistic husband.

Dani took a seat by Detective Monroe. Sal chose to stand by the door, his large frame and commanding presence overwhelming in the close room.

Monroe spoke into the microphone, listing the names of those present, the date, the time.

Brooks glared at her, shifted in his chair. "You've got no reason to bring me in here this way. No reason at all."

His lawyer placed a restraining hand on Brooks's arm.

"Oh, I think we have plenty of reason," Monroe said and tapped a sheaf of papers on the small, scarred table. "We have records of funds transferred from your account to an officer in the Atlanta P.D. We have a written deposition from said officer saying how you paid him to look the other way about your monitor records."

"You can't trust anything a dirty cop like Washington says. He'd sell out his own mother if the price was right."

"That's funny." Monroe turned to Dani. "Deputy District Attorney Barclay, did you hear me say that the cop's name was Washington?"

"No, I didn't."

"I wonder, then, how Mr. Brooks here knew the name of the cop."

She scratched her head in mock perplexity. "I don't know. Unless he was the one who paid off Officer Washington."

Monroe shifted his gaze back to Brooks. "You're right about one thing. You can't trust a dirty cop. You should have thought about that before you teamed up with Washington."

Dani spoke. "You can do yourself some good, Mr. Brooks, if you tell us who put you up to this."

"I've got nothing to say to you." He nodded in Monroe's direction. "Or to him."

"We think someone gave you the security code to Ms. Barclay's apartment," Monroe said as though Brooks hadn't said anything. "Tell us how that person communicated with you."

"What makes you think I didn't do this on my own? And, mind you, I'm not saying I had anything to do with it." Brooks glared at his lawyer, who tried to interrupt.

"It's a theory we're working with," Dani said, her gaze

never leaving his. "You like to break things, like your wife's bones, so that fits, but you also like to be there. You like to see your victim. I wasn't there that night, so you couldn't see what reaction I had, if any."

"You're so smart, Ms. D.D.A.," Brooks said with ill-concealed venom. "Maybe you'd better think about this. Someone out there hates you. Someone even smarter than me."

"Doesn't take too much intelligence to be smarter than an abuser like you," Sal put in.

The lawyer tossed an angry look Sal's way. "Who's he and what's he doing here?"

"He has departmental permission to be here," Monroe said.

Brooks started to laugh. "I get it. He's one of her body-guards. Someone's got you really scared, don't they, to make you hire two goons to watch your back?"

Dani darted a quick look at Sal, but he appeared unconcerned by Brooks's insult. He only folded his thick arms across his chest and managed to look more intimidating than ever.

"I've got nothing more to say to you," Brooks said. "I'd stand, but, as you see, I'm sort of tied up at the moment."

No one laughed at his lame joke.

Dani stood. "You're going away for a long time. For Stephanie's sake, as well as society's, I couldn't be happier."

"You'll get yours," Brooks said. "And I'll be there cheering."

A chill brushed over her, and she did her best to ignore it. No one was going to get to her, not with Jake and Sal guarding her.

"Don't pay him no nevermind," Sal said as they walked back to his truck. "He's a lowlife."

"One of the nastiest," Dani agreed. "If you could see the pictures of his wife after the last beating he gave her..."

She shook her head, the memory of those horrific pictures tightening her lips. "I've seen some pretty terrible stuff on this job, but those gave me nightmares." Then she thought of what Sal must have witnessed in the war. "I'm sorry. You must have your own share of nightmare-causing pictures."

"That I do. But if I'm ever able to look at a picture of a woman beaten half to death by her husband and not feel something, I'll know that I've lost my humanity."

She liked Sal for many reasons, not the least of which was his ability to roll with the punches and to have fun while doing it, but his compassion for a woman he'd never even met constricted her throat. At the same time, tears burned the backs of her eyelids. Jake and Sal were alike in so many ways, but it was Jake who set her heart to racing.

In the truck, Dani angled to face him. "I'm pretty lucky to have you on my side."

"You've got Jake. Now you've got me." His grin lightened the atmosphere. "You're right—you're pretty lucky."

Dani had cause to think on Sal's words over the next few days. Brooks was arraigned for the vandalism and threats made against a D.D.A.

The judge, Harold Mastoff, known as Hang 'Em Harry, refused to grant bail. Over the protests of his lawyer, Brooks was remanded to custody.

Dani did a little happy dance in her head. To the reporters, she maintained a dignified decorum, saying only that she was gratified to "see justice done."

"Does the vandalism of your apartment mean you will ease up on the other charges against Jerry Brooks?" one reporter asked.

Dani stopped her descent of the courthouse stairs and turned to face Taryn Starks, a reporter determined to make a name for herself, often at the expense of the truth. Starks was the worst kind of journalist, sensationalizing stories, badgering victims. Because of Jerry Brooks's seat on the city council, the reporter had hounded Stephanie Brooks until she had been reduced to tears.

"Absolutely not. Stephanie Brooks deserves her day in court. And she'll get it. The charges of spousal abuse will take precedence over any other charges, and our office will bring the full force of its authority to see that she receives justice. Mr. Brooks's ill-advised vandalism and threats against me will be dealt with in a separate action."

"What are your feelings about the defendant in this case?" Starks persisted.

"What are *your* feelings about a man who beats his wife until she can't stand and has to be taken to the hospital on a stretcher?" She turned the reporter's words back on her. "Now, if you'll excuse me, I have work to do. I suggest you do the same rather than taking up both our time on questions that are irrelevant at best and verging on malicious."

Jake and Sal had stood a discreet distance away while Dani was being questioned by the reporters. Now they joined her.

"You were great," Jake said.

Dani hunched a shoulder, embarrassed at the praise. "Thanks to you and Detective Monroe, I had all the evidence I needed to have Brooks bound over for trial. All I did was present it."

Jake wrapped an arm around her. "You dealt with Brooks and you handled that reporter." His hard tone made it clear just what he thought of Taryn Starks.

Dani couldn't repress a grimace at the woman's name. Starks had been hounding her ever since the reporter's arrival in Atlanta three years ago. For some reason, she had zeroed in on Dani, determined to make her appear both foolish and ineffective. As far as Dani knew, she'd never offended the woman. Until today.

"She's jealous of you," Sal said, speaking for the first time. "You have it all. Looks. Intelligence. Competence. She's a second-rater, and she knows it."

A thoughtful expression crossed Jake's face.

"You don't think she's connected with the stalking, do you?" Dani asked.

"We can't afford to rule out anyone. Least of all a woman who's clearly out to make you look bad. Sal's right. Starks is jealous. Jealousy can be a powerful motive."

With that, Dani's ebullient mood vanished. When the stalking had started, she couldn't imagine who hated her to such an extent. Now, it seemed, she had too many people who wished her ill.

Sal helped her into the front seat of Jake's Jeep. "Where to now?"

"The office," Dani said. "I've got cases to prepare."

"I'll drop you two off." Jake headed the Jeep to the city building.

With Sal, Dani returned to her office. She had the beginning of a tension headache. She ignored it and wished she could as easily ignore the pain that so many people in her life appeared to have reason to wish her ill.

She understood why Brooks and Newton disliked or even hated her, but she was still struggling to wrap her mind around the fact that her coworkers and even a reporter she barely knew seemed to take glee in her difficulties. What had she done to them?

Lately, she scarcely recognized herself. She looked at everyone differently, with a suspicion born of fear. That wasn't who she wanted to be. The stalker had taken so much from her already. He had terrorized her with his gruesome gifts, driven her from her home, vandalized her belongings. Now he was taking away her trust in others, as well.

What more could he take?

The answer came swiftly: her life.

* * *

Jake had work of his own to do, work that he didn't want to involve Dani in. Leaving her, even with Sal, was one of the hardest things he'd ever done, but he felt time slipping through his fingers. Tension edged along his skin as a sense of urgency grew stronger.

Instinct told him that the stalker had an endgame in mind, a game that Dani wouldn't survive, and each day that passed without answers was another day she was in danger. There was nothing more important than keeping her safe.

Nothing he'd ever experienced compared with his feelings for her. If he lost her… He didn't go there. He wouldn't lose her. He had to be fast enough, strong enough, clever enough to stop the madman who had Dani in his sights.

Jake started with a search of unidentified female bodies from four years ago. He knew the police had done a similar search, but they hadn't believed that Madeline Barclay had met with foul play and had little reason to do a follow-up. The consensus at the time of her disappearance was that she had taken off for reasons of her own.

The game had changed, at least as far as Jake was concerned. A call to Shelley was the first order of business.

Briefly, he explained the circumstances of the disappearance.

"You think this has something to do with what's happening to Dani now?" Shelley asked, clearly skeptical.

"I think it has everything to do with it."

"What's the connection?"

"I don't know, but it seems too much of a coincidence that the mother disappears, then, a few years later, the daughter is stalked and receives a dead fish on the anniversary of her mother's disappearance."

Jake had never liked coincidences. In the complex scheme of life, they occurred, of course, but he always felt compelled to look at where the threads crossed, whether it was truly random, or if a larger design were at work, a pattern that could be detected only when you followed those individual threads back to the source.

"Use your computer magic and see what you can find about any unidentified women around fifty years of age four years ago."

"Okay, big brother. I know enough to trust your hunches."

Jake did some digging of his own. A visit to the county coroner proved unfruitful.

"Of course we keep records," an assistant said somewhat testily. "But you're asking me to go back four years." He gestured around him. "A lot of bodies have come and gone in that period."

"Just do your best. I'll get back to you."

Two days later, Shelley called. "There's no record of a body of a woman of Madeline Barclay's description. Anywhere." She paused. "What's this about, Jake?"

"You'll know when I do."

The county coroner's office reported the same thing.

Jake wasn't surprised by the negative results. He'd suspected that, but he'd had to make sure. He had his own idea of what had happened to Dani's mother.

"I'm heading to Belle Terre," he told Dani early that afternoon. "I need to talk with your father about your mother's disappearance." He didn't tell Dani what he believed had happened to Madeline Barclay. Not yet.

Believing her mother had just taken off was one thing; learning that she was dead was another one entirely. He wouldn't put Dani through that until he had concrete proof that her mother was dead.

She stood. "I'll go with you."

Jake held up a hand. "I think your father might be willing to talk more freely if you weren't there."

"Maybe you're right." She didn't sound happy about it, but she took her seat.

"I promise to tell you if I find out anything." He bent as though to brush a kiss across her brow, then stopped himself.

"I'll be here."

The trip to the Barclay home could be measured in more than mere distance. Every mile emphasized the differences between Dani's upbringing and his own. Dani had grown up with riding lessons and cotillions, trips to Europe and designer clothes. His childhood was forged in the harsh realities of the projects, where every day was a test of survival, where he'd fought to steer clear of gangbangers and drug pushers, hustlers and thieves.

He'd pulled himself and Shelley out of the abyss of poverty and ignorance with sheer will and a burning desire to make something out of himself. He put those memories behind him and focused on what he needed to do. Putting Senator Barclay through the pain of reliving what must be hurtful memories wasn't something he looked forward to, but it couldn't be helped.

If he was right, Madeline Barclay's disappearance was the root of Dani's stalking.

The senator welcomed him, a curious look on his distinguished face. "Rabb. What can I do for you?"

"Sir, I've got some questions for you. They won't be easy."

The senator swept a hand toward the library. "Come in. Let's make ourselves comfortable."

Once seated in an overstuffed chair, the older man said, "Now, tell me what it is I can help you with."

"It's about your wife's disappearance."

Sorrow shadowed the senator's face. "I don't talk about that time. Ever."

"I understand. But it may have something to do with what's happening to Dani now."

"I don't see the connection."

"What do you remember of that day?"

"Madeline dressed for the city, told me she was meeting Dani for breakfast, then friends for lunch. That wasn't unusual. She frequently drove to the city, for lunch, shopping, one of her charity meetings. Later, when the police questioned her friends, the women said that Madeline never showed up. Never even called. That wasn't like her. Madeline was a stickler for manners."

"Do you know anything about other appointments she might have had that day?"

If anything, the expression on the senator's face grew even more regretful. "Later, I learned from the private detectives I'd hired that she had an appointment with an oncologist. She never said a word to me about it, never gave a hint that anything was wrong." He shook his head as though to wipe away painful memories. "I could only guess that she didn't want to put Dani and me through a long, drawn-out illness." He coughed, his voice rough and hoarse. "Why didn't she know that I would have been by her side, no matter what?"

"I'm sure she did, Senator."

"Then why? Why leave the way she did?"

"Maybe she didn't have a choice."

"You're thinking someone kidnapped her."

Jake didn't know how else to say the next words. "I think someone killed her."

"Why? Madeline didn't have an enemy in the world. Everyone who knew her loved her."

"Are you so sure?"

"Of course. She was a true Southern lady. More than that, though, she cared about others. There wasn't a charity that she didn't contribute to and work for. She always said we were blessed and she wanted to give something back."

Like Dani. Jake had a feeling that he would have liked Madeline Barclay very much.

"Dani told me that your wife didn't approve of her relationship with Wingate."

"Madeline never thought Wingate was good enough for Dani. It's a natural enough thing. Most parents don't think the man who wants to marry their daughter is good enough for her."

"Had she felt that way about other men in Dani's life?"

The senator rubbed his chin. "Dani never went out much. She was always too focused on her studies, then her career. Her mother and I tried to get her to socialize, to get out more, but she said that when she found the right man, she'd know it, and until then she was content as she was. That's why her relationship with Victor took us by surprise."

"How do you feel about Wingate?"

"I like him well enough. He's ambitious, but I'm the last to hold that against a man. To tell the truth, he reminds me of myself thirty years ago. Eager. Too much so, perhaps."

"Did you ever feel that he was using his relationship with Dani to get to you?"

"You mean that he wanted me to give him a leg up? Sure. Like I said, the man's ambitious. But that's not a sin. If it were, half of Washington would be in trouble." The senator directed a shrewd look Jake's way. "You can't think he had anything to do with Madeline taking off as she did."

"I don't think your wife took off at all. I think she's buried, probably not too far from here."

The senator stood, then sank slowly back into his chair. Within moments, he'd aged a decade. His face had grayed, his body seeming to have shrunk in on itself. "I guess I always suspected she was dead. But I never wanted to believe it. I avoided saying the words aloud, afraid that that would make them true." He gave a humorless laugh. "I haven't told Dani, couldn't even say the words if I wanted to. Sometimes I'd look at her and know she wanted to talk about what had happened to her mother, but I couldn't. I just couldn't." He shook his head at his own weakness. "Pathetic, isn't it?"

"Human." Jake understood the older man's reluctance to talk about something so painful all too well. Hadn't he been avoiding that very thing for over a year? Because he'd been afraid, afraid of what he'd reveal, afraid of what he'd learn about himself.

"What is it you want me to do?"

"I want you to go through your wife's diaries, journals, any scraps of paper you can find. See if you can find anything about that last week and days."

A baffled expression on the senator's face, he nodded. "What are you going to do?"

"I'm going to do a little research of my own."

Thirty minutes later, he was at the county hall of records, attacking files with the determination of a treasure hunter searching for gold. Rather than precious metal, though, he dug for secrets, for answers, for truth.

Going through the computerized records, he followed the trail. The information had been buried deep. Someone skilled at computers had done a very good job of covering his tracks. If Jake hadn't been looking specifically for it, he'd have missed it.

Twenty years ago, a Mick Devane had petitioned the state to change his name, and with that, Victor Wingate had been born. A further check into Devane's background showed his date and place of birth. It wasn't too much of a leap to surmise how Devane, now Wingate, had enrolled in Harvard and invented the background he'd told Dani.

Jake made a quick call to Shelley, asked her to check Harvard's records. His computer skills were passable, but Shelley's were outstanding. What she couldn't find wasn't worth finding.

He drove to Dani's office, anxious to share what he'd

learned. When Shelley called, confirming his guess, he wasn't surprised.

"I have you now," he said, addressing the individual who had been making Dani's life a misery. "I have you now."

Fury roared through Jake at what Dani and her father had been put through in not knowing what had happened to Madeline Barclay. It was the cruelest form of torture, the uncertainty as to her fate.

Jake white-knuckled the steering wheel, as though all his anger could be absorbed by the act. Patience, he reminded himself. He would bring Dani and her father the peace of mind they deserved and make the person responsible pay.

"Dani. I need to see you. There's something you need to know." Victor's voice came over the line, the urgency of it at odds with his usual smooth tone.

"I have work. Can it wait?"

"No." His voice lowered. "I have information about your stalker."

Dani's hand tightened around her phone. "When and where should we meet?"

"One problem—my source is the nervous type. He won't agree to meet if you bring your bodyguard."

She didn't have to think about it. "No."

"Think about it," Victor wheedled. "You want to put an end to the stalking, don't you? My source can give you the ammo you need to do just that."

"Just who is your source?"

"Not over the phone." Victor's voice took on a hint of desperation. "I went out on a limb for you, Dani. If you don't show up, I'm going to take some grief." He waited a beat. "We meant something to each other at one time," he said and let that sink in.

He was right, and she felt herself weakening for a moment. Then she hardened her resolve. "Don't play the relationship card."

"I'm just reminding you of what we had once. What we could have again, if you'd give us a chance."

"It's over. I'm sorry."

"I figured you'd say that. But I still want to help you. For old times' sake." And with that, he was the friend she had known and relied on, the man who had helped her through the worst time of her life.

"What if I tell my bodyguard to stay in the car while I talk with you and your source?"

"He'll think it's a setup. He's more than a bit paranoid."

Dani ran through scenarios. She thought of Jake's reaction if she were to ditch Sal. The last thing she wanted was to cause problems between the two men. "I'm sorry, Victor. I can't come. If you want to come here—"

"That's not possible," he was practically shouting now. More quietly, he added, "You're making a mistake."

"If I am, it's mine to make."

Dani hung up the phone, convinced she'd made the right choice. She didn't have anything to fear from Victor, but going out alone to meet an unknown source was more than foolish. It was stupid.

She'd never been stupid.

Determinedly, she put the incident out of her mind and got back to work. With the new charges against Brooks, she had added another case to her already heavy caseload.

When the phone chirped, she checked the ID and saw it was Victor. She couldn't deal with any more of his pleas or demands, not now, and turned off the phone.

If she didn't get the brief she was working on finished, she risked annoying the judge. The brief needed to be perfect, *t*'s crossed and *i*'s dotted. Judge Prescott was a stickler for citing case law for every point raised.

The concentration required kept her mind off Victor and his badgering.

At six, a timid knock sounded on the door.

Dani called out a distracted "Come in."

"I'm sorry to bother you, Ms. Barclay—I mean Dani," Clariss began, "but Mr. Rabb called. He wants you to meet him at Mr. Brooks's apartment. He said there's something there you have to see."

"Why didn't he call me on my cell?"

"He said you weren't picking up."

Her own fault. She'd never turned the phone back on. "Where's Mr. Santonni?"

"He told me to tell you that he had to step out and check on something for Mr. Rabb. He said he'd be back in a few minutes."

Dani debated. "Call Mr. Rabb back. Ask him if I can meet him in an hour."

Clariss cleared her throat. "I can't do that. He said he was watching someone and couldn't alert them. If the phone rings…"

"I get it. Did he say anything else?"

Clariss looked confused. "Anything else… Oh, he did say something, but it sounded sort of strange."

"What was it?"

"He said to tell you *grace*."

"Thank you." Dani gathered up her purse. "Would you please call me a cab?"

"Right away."

Clariss scurried off, leaving Dani to tidy up her paperwork. She'd finish the brief later tonight.

By the time the cab arrived, Dani was waiting on the front steps of the city building. She climbed into the backseat and gave the cabbie the address.

"You sure, ma'am? That's a bad part of town."

"I'm sure."

What had Jake found? And who was he watching? Anticipation raced along her nerves as she wondered if this would put an end to the stalking.

When the cab pulled up outside Brooks's building, an old hotel that had seen better days and was now operated on a pay-by-the-week basis, Dani pulled some bills from her purse and handed them to the cabbie.

"You want me to wait for you?"

She shook her head. "No, thank you." Jake would see her home.

Inside, she crossed the once grand front lobby, now shabby, its velvet drapes and carpet dingy, the windows dirt-streaked, and thought of how Jerry Brooks had fallen. He and Stephanie had once had a beautiful home. With his arrest and the forfeiture of his assets to pay his bond, he had been reduced to living in this place.

There was no clerk at the front desk. She gave the ancient elevator a dubious look, then decided to take the stairs.

On the third floor, she walked down the hallway until she found the number of Brooks's room.

She pushed on the door. "Jake?"

There was silence. And then, "Surprise."

"Victor?"

Her senses went on alert, but she felt no real alarm. After all, Clariss had given the code word. Maybe Jake had arranged for Victor to meet them here.

"You were expecting your bodyguard, perhaps?"

She nodded.

"That's the surprise. He's not coming. You got me instead." Victor's eyes held a maniacal glee, unsuited to the situation.

"I don't understand."

"But you will, Dani darling. You will."

He advanced toward her.

She took an instinctive step backward. Another.

He lunged for her, yanking her toward him. A sharp prick stung her arm.

She felt herself falling. Falling, falling, falling. Until there was only blackness.

ELEVEN

"Where is she?"

Jake found Sal slumped behind a desk in Dani's office. His friend looked groggy, disoriented. If Jake hadn't known better, he'd have said that Sal was drugged, but that was impossible. Sal had lost a younger brother to drugs. He never touched anything stronger than the mildest painkiller.

"Wh...what?"

"Dani. Where is she?"

Sal shook himself as though to dispel whatever drug was still inside him. "I don't know."

Take it easy, Jake told himself. Unable to reach either Dani or Sal on their cell phones, he'd raced to the city building, only to find Dani missing and Sal out of it.

With an effort, Sal got to his feet. "I'm sorry, man. I don't know what happened. The last thing I remember was that I was drinking some tea. The little secretary said how she was brewing a pot and asked if I'd like some. Chamomile with honey. I said yes and..." He ended with a shrug.

"Clariss? Are you saying she drugged you?"

"I don't know." Sal's words were still slurred, his eyes glassy. "She's a little bit of a thing with no reason to hurt me."

"Unless she wanted you out of the way so that she could get to Dani."

"Why?"

"She could be another pawn. We've all been played.

Dani. Newton. Brooks. Me." It hurt his throat to give voice to the words, to his failure to keep Dani safe.

Sal shook his head, more in an attempt to clear it than to deny Jake's words. "I'm not following."

"It doesn't matter. We've got to find Dani."

Jake looked around. Nothing appeared out of place. Dani's desk was tidy, as it always was, the computer shut down, any files she might have been working on presumably locked away.

"Think," Jake ordered. "What were you doing before you drank the tea?"

"I was going back through the detective's notes on the Madeline Barclay case. It doesn't make sense that nothing ever turned up."

"Unless she was dead, buried someplace where she'd never be found."

"That's what you've thought all along, isn't it? That she's been dead these four years. Not missing."

Jake nodded. "It's the only thing that makes sense."

"Then who? And why?"

"I'll tell you on the way."

"On the way where?"

"You'll see."

Jake drove like a madman. Late-afternoon traffic was heavy, but he maneuvered the Jeep in and out of lanes.

"If you want to kill us both, there're easier ways," Sal said mildly.

"Shut up and listen." Jake outlined what he'd found out. He had Sal's full attention now.

"It's Wingate? He's the one behind it all?" Sal's skepticism was plain. "The way you described him, he sounded like a weak sister."

"He's far from that. He's clever, cunning and a master manipulator. Wingate wanted Dani. Four years ago, when her mother threatened to break up their relationship, Wingate got rid of her. That accomplished two things. First, it removed the barrier that stood between him and Dani. Second, it made Dani turn to him. For comfort. Support. And that's exactly what she did. Maybe she was even falling in love with him a little bit."

"Can't blame her," Sal put in. "She was hurting. Her daddy was hurting, too, and probably couldn't give her what she needed right then."

"I don't blame Dani." Never Dani. Jake put the blame squarely where it belonged. On Victor Wingate's head. "She was grateful, and he used it to play her."

"Then she smartened up and sent him packing." Sal took up the story.

"Yeah. From what she told me, he got possessive, started trying to control her life."

"What about all the business with Newton and Brooks?" The blurriness had vanished from Sal's gaze, his expression now grimly focused.

"Wingate contacted them, being careful that it couldn't be traced back to him. He told Newton about Dani's allergy to peanuts. He set it up so Newton could get hired on with the caterer for the awards night."

"And Brooks?" Sal wondered.

"Brooks took a bit more doing. Wingate did his homework and found out about Brooks and Washington's relationship. He also had to find a way around Dani's security system."

"How'd he manage that?"

"I found out that before Devane turned himself into Wingate he worked at a security outfit, installing new security systems, upgrading old ones. Bypassing Dani's security would have been child's play for him."

"You never told me where we're heading."

The worry in Sal's voice didn't begin to match that which festered in Jake's gut. Picture after picture of Wingate holding Dani captive swirled in his mind, causing his desperation to soar. "Where it all began."

"Good. You're coming around."

Dani awoke slowly, head throbbing and mind muzzy. She looked down to find her wrists bound to the arms of an old wooden chair. Her gaze traveled around the room, taking in the yellowed wallpaper, the carpet so worn that only the pad was visible in places.

"What happened? How did I get here?"

Victor bestowed a smile upon her. "I brought you here. It wasn't difficult. I took you down the freight elevator, carried you to the car, then drove here."

"Why?" The aftereffects of the drug he'd administered made her slow, her reasoning powers sluggish.

"Don't you get it?" Victor shook his head in mock disappointment. "I'd thought better of you. I'm the one you've been looking for. 'The evil stalker.'" He made air quotes around the words. They should have been funny coming from mild-mannered Victor, but they weren't. His normally pleasant features had twisted into something malevolent.

Dani tried to wrap her mind around his words. As her confusion cleared and understanding came, the air felt as if all the oxygen had been sucked out of it.

Victor? He was the stalker? The last thing she remembered was seeing Victor in the apartment where Jerry Brooks had lived. She'd been startled, as she'd thought she was meeting Jake there. Before she could register what was happening, Victor had pricked her arm with something, and she was out cold.

She wasn't afraid. Fear hadn't yet punctured the numbness that enveloped her. This was a man she'd known more than four years, a man she considered a friend and basically honest, if a trifle weak.

"How did you know I'd be at Brooks's apartment?"

"Think it through," he said patiently. "I'm sure you'll get it."

"Clariss said that Jake called and told me to meet him there," she said, replaying the series of events. "But you couldn't have known that. You couldn't have known he wouldn't have been able to reach me."

"Of course I knew. I played you, Dani. I knew if I kept pestering you to meet me that you'd turn off your phone. You're so predictable." He made a tsking sound. "Whenever you have your nose in a case, everything else takes second place and you turn off your phone. I should know. I took second place to your work plenty of times."

He was right. He had played her. And she'd fallen into the trap.

"I grew up in this house." Victor spread his hands, taking in the faded wallpaper, the sagging floor, the patched walls, the smell of misery that clung to it. "Not quite what you're accustomed to, is it, darling?"

She fought against the residual effects of the drug and struggled to stay focused. "I thought you were raised in Mississippi." The stories Victor had told were of a genteel upbringing in one of the stately homes that still dotted the Mississippi landscape, then on to prep school, college and law school.

"I lied. About everything," Victor said, sounding almost cheerful. "I even lied about my name. It's Mick. Mick Devane."

"Why? Why lie about who you are?"

Victor raised his hand, slapped her, hard, across the face. Bruising agony. She fought her way through it.

"Do you think a woman like you would have given me a second glance if she knew I'd been raised in this Podunk town by a mother who took in washing to make the rent? You'd have turned up that cute little nose of yours and run in the other direction."

"None of that would have mattered."

He slapped her again. Her head snapped back. A red haze misted her vision, and she tasted blood where she'd bitten her lip.

"Of course it matters. I would never have gotten into law school if the officials had known about my background. So I reinvented myself. I became Victor Wingate. I found the name in a history book. I liked it, so I had my name changed legally. The rest I accomplished with superior, if I do say so myself, computer skills. It's amazing what you can do with a few keystrokes and a little imagination."

"So you reinvented yourself. Others have done it. It didn't turn them into stalkers." She softened her voice. "You terrified me, Victor. I thought we were friends."

"Friends? You think I wanted friendship from you?" He turned the word into something ugly. "Don't you get it? I had to have you so scared that you'd turn to me, lean on me. Just like you did before."

"Before?" Then a terrible truth hit her, and she understood. "My mother."

"Now you're getting it," he said, beaming with approval. "Yes, the dearly departed Madeline Barclay. Your mother was smarter than I gave her credit for. She found out about Mick Devane. She ordered me to tell you the truth myself or she would."

Dani had always prided herself on her ability to read others. Victor had completely fooled her. Why hadn't she seen him for who he was, what he was? Had she been so blinded by the idea of love that she'd failed to see the man beneath the easy charm and handsome features?

Only her mother had looked beneath the smooth and polished surface and seen the evil inside.

Somehow, Jake would find her. She had to believe that. All she had to do was buy time. Keep Victor talking.

"How did she find out?"

"It seems one of her friends grew up not far from here. She'd seen me at a party you'd invited me to and asked your mother about me. From there, it didn't take long for Madeline to put the pieces together and trace me here."

Dani was putting a few pieces together herself, and what she came up with turned her voice hollow with horror. "You killed her. Didn't you?"

"That I did." His mouth curled into a smirk. "You could say that I was doing her a favor. She had cancer, you know. That's where she was heading that day, to see her doctor. I'd been following her for a while and was curious when I saw her enter the doctor's office. I chatted up the receptionist. You'd be surprised what you can learn, like when a patient is scheduled to return. All I had to do was pretend to be a worried son, distraught that his sick mother hadn't confided in him.

"I arranged to meet your dear old Maddie for coffee before her appointment. I told her that I was going to come clean and tell you everything, but that I needed to talk with her first. I slipped something into her cup, helped her out of the restaurant and into my car.

"I hacked into her doctor's records. She had three years to live, five at the most. I saved her and you and your precious daddy all those years of agony of watching her slowly waste away and die."

He was a monster. Every word was a red-hot brand that filled her with anguish. Victor knew it and was deliberately pouring acid into the wounds he'd inflicted. Her chest grew tight; she felt perspiration bead her face as she struggled to accept that she had once thought of marrying this man.

"You robbed her of that time, however short it was, with our family. You robbed us all. You made me doubt her love for me." Dani gave him a look of such loathing that she was surprised he didn't melt from the hatred in it. "You're despicable."

He ignored that. "I wanted you from the first time I set eyes on you," he said, and his voice took on a dreamy quality. "You were everything I looked for in a woman. Poised. Beautiful. Smart. From a good family with an impeccable pedigree. You were like a Thoroughbred, just waiting for the right owner."

Revulsion filled her at the image of Victor owning her.

Victor now seemed detached from his surroundings, as though he'd drifted into a surreal state. "Pedigree is everything. Did you know that?" He shook his head at his own question. "Why should you? You were born with a silver spoon in your mouth and a genealogy that could be traced back to the *Mayflower*. You never gave it a thought, never would have looked at me, a poor kid who couldn't trace his family back further than some dirt-poor sharecroppers."

"It's what a person is on the inside that matters. It's the only thing that matters." She thought of Jake, pulling his sister and himself out of poverty and the hopelessness that had been their life. He had no fancy pedigree that Victor put such stock in. No, Jake had something far more important. Faith. Integrity. Courage.

"Don't patronize me. You wouldn't have given me the time of day if you knew the truth about me."

He was right about that, but not in the way he meant. If she'd known what kind of man he was—a cold, calculating murderer—she would have done just as he'd said and run in the opposite direction as fast as her legs could carry her.

Unable to help herself, her gaze slid to the knife sheathed at his waist. She couldn't tear her eyes away from the lethal-looking object.

He followed her gaze. "Ah, I see you like my plaything." He clasped the hilt of the knife with his right hand. "It was a gift to myself when I passed the bar. It has a history, you know. It's said that this knife belonged to a Southern gentleman and that he used it to slit the throat of a Yankee who invaded his home." Victor studied her.

"I'm frightening you, aren't I?"

She thought about denying it, then nodded. If she admitted to being frightened, he was more likely to keep talking, to feel a sense of power.

Her mouth went dry. At the same time, she struggled to breathe. She recognized the beginnings of an asthma attack. She wet her lips. "My purse…inhaler."

He picked up her purse, pulled the inhaler from it, then dropped it on the floor and kicked it aside. "Things could have been so good for us, if you'd only given me a chance."

Dani's breathing grew more irregular. "I did give you a chance, Victor," she said in a husky voice. "It didn't work out. That's no reason to kill me."

"I hadn't planned on killing you. I was going to marry you and have the perfect life. But it's too late for that." He pointed to a grime-streaked window.

"She's right out there. I had to bury her where no one would find her. This little piece of nothing seemed the perfect place for the high-and-mighty Madeline Barclay. Oh, how she loved holding my past over me."

"All my mother asked you to do was to tell the truth." Each word was an effort now. What kind of man killed an innocent woman because she'd found out a few unpalatable facts about him? She answered her own question: a madman. Victor was certainly insane, and that made him more dangerous than ever.

Her throat felt as if it was closing. *Breathe slowly. Quietly. Don't let him frighten you any more than he already has.* Deliberately, she calmed her breathing, taking shallow breaths that didn't rattle in her chest.

"It didn't work out because we weren't right for each other," she said in what she hoped was a reasonable-sounding voice. "It had nothing to do with my mother. I wanted to work. I needed to work. You wanted a different kind of woman. I couldn't be her."

"I wanted you. It was you from the first moment I saw you. Only you. We could have traveled, seen the Arc de Triomphe or the great museums of Italy, anywhere you wanted to go. I would have given you the world, laid it at your feet. We could have lived anywhere, had everything we ever wanted."

"Only I didn't want the world," she said softly. Not Victor's kind of world, where money reigned and appearances mattered more than substance. Never that. "I wanted to make a difference in the world. For the world. You never understood that."

"You and that job of yours. It wasn't worthy of you."

"Any job is worthy if you do it with honesty and integrity."

He made a disgusted sound. "Then there was that ridiculous faith of yours. You were always spouting it. Faith doesn't get you anywhere. My mama prayed day and night, got calluses on her knees for all her prayers, and all it ever got her was rough hands and a sore back as she did other people's wash. She said if we had enough faith that the Lord would provide."

"She was right," Dani said. She had to have faith that Jake would figure it out, that he would find her. In the meantime, she had to do her part, to keep Victor bragging about his cleverness so that he wouldn't use that knife on her.

Was that how he'd killed her mother? A shudder rippled through Dani. Her mother had been fragile and delicate; she would never have been able to fend off a determined Victor.

Dani reminded herself that she was neither fragile nor delicate. She'd had defense training. If only she could get her hands loose...

Surreptitiously, she wiggled her fingers, testing the knots.

It seemed as though Victor had taken cruel pleasure in tying the knots as tightly as possible.

"You won't get free," he said, reading her mind.

"But you could set me free," she said, softening her voice. "You could make all this right by untying me and letting me go. It's not too late."

His harsh laugh told her just how unlikely that was to occur. She looked into his eyes. And saw her fate.

"And your mama? What am I to do about her? Please don't bother telling me that you won't tell anyone what I did with her."

He was right. Even if she convinced him that he might escape charges for the stalking and kidnapping, there was her mother's murder. A tiny sob escaped. Unbelievable pain clenched her heart.

Oh, Mama. I thought you'd run off all those years ago. I thought you didn't love me. And all this time, you were here. You died trying to protect me, and I never knew. Forgive me.

"Don't bother crying for her. I have to hand it to her, though." Victor gave an admiring shake of his head. "She didn't plead, didn't beg. I think she knew it wouldn't make any difference. She was a lady right to the end, all dignity and breeding and looking down that royal nose of hers. Do you know I used to hate the way she looked at me, as though I were nothing?"

"Turns out she was right, wasn't she?"

The slap stunned Dani and, for a moment, she must have passed out. When she regained consciousness, she felt a trickle of blood at the corner of her mouth. Her breathing had grown increasingly labored.

If Victor kept her here much longer, he wouldn't have to bother using the knife. He could just let the asthma take her.

No!

"What about Newton and Brooks? Were they part of your plan?"

"It was ridiculously easy to manipulate them. They wanted nothing more than to get even with you. All I did was give them a helping hand. I sent an email to Newton, telling her of your peanut allergy. I told her just how much to use. I couldn't have her killing you. I only wanted you to be sick."

"Sick and vulnerable, so I'd turn to you."

"That's right," he said, in the manner of a teacher encouraging a slow pupil. "I had everything planned. Did you notice that the fish arrived on the anniversary of the day your mother disappeared?"

"You did that on purpose?" Horror at his deviousness welled inside her. How could she not have seen the evil inside of him?

"Of course."

"But your plan didn't work." *Careful,* she cautioned herself. *Don't make him angry.* "I didn't turn to you."

Victor's face darkened. "No. You had your bodyguard. He was always around, always interfering."

"And Brooks?"

"I hacked into your building's security program and bypassed the security code to the outside door and to your apartment door." An ugly smirk crossed Victor's face. "Brooks didn't even need a key. All he had to do was waltz in the front door while an out-of-work actor was playing the part of a cop and distracting the doorman."

"And you wiped the video feed."

"Of course. Child's play." He shot her a playful look. "You really ought to live in a building with a better security system." He snapped his fingers. "Oh, that's right. It doesn't matter anymore. You won't be needing it. Just like you won't be needing your two bodyguards."

Sal had been at the office with her. "Sal? What did you do to him?"

"He'll be out for a little while. Groggy but none the worse for wear."

Thank goodness for that. "And Jake?" *Please, Lord,* she prayed, *let Jake be all right.*

"Ah, yes, your watchdog. I have plans for him." Victor leaned over, stroked her cheek.

Repelled by his touch, she pulled away. "Leave Jake out of this."

"So brave," Victor murmured and held the knife to her throat.

Dani refused to close her eyes; she waited for the knife to pierce her skin, all the while breathing in the cold scent of her own terror.

He studied her face and must have seen the resolve in her eyes. "I knew you were falling for him. He's a nobody, but you chose him over me. For that alone, you'll pay." He grabbed a handful of her hair, yanked it. "Don't worry. Your precious Jake is safe. For now."

She sagged in relief.

"Who knows, though? An accident may befall him at a future date." Victor shook his head in mock sorrow. "The way he drives that big black Jeep of his—it's just an accident waiting to happen." His lips curved when her face bleached of all color.

She wouldn't beg for herself, but she would for Jake. "Please. Jake's done nothing to you."

"He took you from me! He made you fall in love with him." Outrage rimmed Victor's voice, and he rubbed his hands together, as if wiping away something particularly foul. She could actually feel the waves of rage he was emitting.

Was it so obvious? Did Jake know of her feelings for him? A sound at the door filled her with hope, and her heart leaped. Jake. Somehow, he'd found her. She knew he would come.

When Clariss walked in, Dani could only stare. "Clariss? How did you know where I was?" Relief filled her, then terror. Now Victor had two hostages.

It was only then that she understood. If she hadn't been so muddled from whatever drug Victor had given her, she'd have already put it together. Clariss had relayed the supposed message from Jake.

Panic.

She did her best to will it back, but her heart was pounding painfully. She could feel her breathing starting to seize, with the accompanying chill and nausea.

Her secretary walked right up to Victor and put her arms around his neck. "Why, Victor told me, of course."

When Clariss had walked in, Dani believed she was going to be rescued. Now she realized there was no hope of rescue. Jake had no idea where she was. She had to save herself. She had to take what she'd been given and make the best of it.

She had a hysterical desire to laugh. She was bound to a chair, growing weaker by the moment. All she could do was keep Victor and Clariss talking.

"You were part of this?" she asked, directing the question to Clariss.

"From the beginning," Clariss said proudly, a cool glaze of contempt hardening her eyes.

Dani looked from one to the other. Victor was the boyfriend Clariss had mentioned but never brought around the office? It made a strange kind of sense. In the past, Clariss had always talked about her boyfriends, bragging about them, blushing when the occasional bouquet of flowers was delivered. With her latest, she had been oddly reluctant to share details.

"I thought we were friends." Clariss's betrayal cut deep. Clariss stared at Dani, her gaze suddenly, shockingly, poisonous. "Friends? Give me a break. You, with your fancy clothes and fancy ways, were always holding your status over me, making me feel inferior."

"That's not true."

"How do you think that dead fish got on your desk without anyone being the wiser? And those letters that arrived without any postmark? It was me. All me." Clariss preened a bit and gave Dani a nasty smile. "You never even thought that your dowdy little secretary was doing it, did you? You were always such a fool. You believed everything I said. You never did give me enough credit. Like how I knew the code word you and your bodyguard devised."

"You were eavesdropping."

"Of course." Clariss sounded smugly proud of herself.

"I did everything I could to help you."

"Like when you refused to write that letter of recommendation I needed to apply to law school?"

"I couldn't lie."

"So holier-than-thou. Well, Dani, how do you feel about me now? Am I good enough for you?" Clariss laughed gaily.

"You were always good enough. It was you who never gave yourself enough credit. You would have gotten into law school eventually. Without lying."

Victor sliced a hand through the air. "Both of you, shut up."

Clariss slanted a sly smile Dani's way. "How're you going to feel when I have your job someday? After Victor helps me get into law school and I graduate, I'm going to be the type of lawyer you never had the guts to be." She pressed against Victor's side. "Isn't that right?"

An uncomfortable look crossed Victor's face. "You don't need to go to law school, baby. You're perfect just the way you are."

"You promised you'd help me once this—" she gestured

toward Dani "—was finished and done with." An edge of doubt had crept into her voice.

"And I will. I'm going to give you the life you always dreamed of."

Dani felt a niggle of hope. Victor was reverting to old patterns, treating Clariss the same way he had treated her, trying to control her. If she could drive a wedge between them, maybe she had a chance of escaping.

"You see, Clariss? Victor doesn't really want to help you. He wants to help himself. And only himself."

"That's not true." The younger woman wound her arm through Victor's, snuggled close to him, oblivious to the distaste on his face. "He's going to help me be a lawyer. Like you. Only better." Her plain face lit with a kind of inner joy.

Despite what the woman had done, Dani felt sorry for her. Clariss was a victim as much as Dani; she just didn't know it. "Victor doesn't like the woman in his life to succeed at anything. He wants to be her rescuer, her controller. That's not love. That's sickness."

Clariss shot her a look of such loathing that Dani wondered why she had never seen the woman's true feelings before. How could she have been so blind? She had seen only what she'd wanted to see. More, she'd seen what Clariss wanted her to see.

"You're being incredibly naive if you believe Victor's going to do anything to get you into law school." Deliberately cruel, Dani added, "You're not his type." She didn't want to hurt the woman, but she had to get through to her.

Dani paused, letting Clariss absorb everything. "As soon as you've outlived your usefulness to him, he'll get rid of you. He has no reason to keep you around. Think on that."

Uncertainty flickered in Clariss's eyes.

Dani seized the opportunity. "Think. Did he ever take you out where you'd be seen together? Or did you always meet in out-of-the-way places? Did he ever introduce you to any of his friends? Did he ever let you talk about him with your girlfriends or were you supposed to keep quiet about your relationship?"

"Victor said it was more romantic if we kept our relationship a secret."

Behind Clariss's back, Victor rolled his eyes, his contempt plain.

"Because it was romantic or because it made it easier for him to get rid of you when he didn't need you anymore?"

Clariss turned to Victor, her eyes pleading with him to deny Dani's charges. "It's not true, is it? Once this is over, we'll be together."

"Of course we will. She's only trying to drive us apart." He skimmed a caressing hand down Clariss's cheek. "She's jealous of you, baby. That's all. She's jealous because you're everything she's not. Ambitious. Smart. Beautiful."

Her face filled with bliss, Clariss leaned into his touch. "But you will help me—"

"Didn't I say I'd help you? I'll put in a good word for you with the dean of the law school." Impatience colored his voice before he tempered it. "After we see to her." The last word was uttered with such hatred that Dani tried to shrink away from him.

She felt herself growing weaker with every breath. The inhaler lay on the floor, not far from where she was tied to the chair, but it might as well have been miles away, for all the good it did her.

Clariss drew herself up, her face set in resolute lines. "Tell me what to do."

"Untie her. We're all going to take a walk outside."

As Clariss worked to undo the knots, Dani whispered, "Victor's a dangerous and cruel man. The only future you have with such a man is more danger and more cruelty. Open your eyes. It's not too late for you."

"You'd say anything to save yourself." But Clariss didn't sound as sure of herself as she had minutes earlier. Her voice quavered, making her sound even younger than Dani knew her to be.

"I'm trying to save you, as well," Dani said and realized that it was true. Clariss could still be saved. It wasn't too late. It wasn't too late for either of them.

"I love him."

With those words, Clariss had sealed her fate. The look in Victor's eyes confirmed it. He had used the young woman's feelings for him even as he was repelled by her.

Dani knew it, just as she knew that Victor would discard the naive secretary. She also knew that it was up to her to save herself. She pretended to faint, slumping forward.

Clariss knelt beside her, shook her.

Dani remained unresponsive.

"She's faking." Victor kicked her, and she couldn't hold back the cry of pain. He kicked her again.

It was no effort to assume the fetal position, the universal pose of the frightened and defeated. Let Victor see what he wanted: a woman who had given up, a woman who would give him no trouble, a woman who was resigned to dying.

When he reared back to kick her a third time, she rolled to the side. Caught by his own momentum, Victor stumbled.

Dani seized her chance and ran to the door. As she started to yank it open, a hard hand grabbed her ankle.

Inexorably, Victor pulled her to him. Dani fought to free herself, using the defensive techniques Shelley and Jake had taught her. With a strength fueled by rage and terror, she kicked out at him.

She was no warrior like Jake and Sal or Shelley, but anyone could be a warrior if the stakes were high enough. She was fighting not only for her life but for Jake's, as well. She would not, could not, let Victor defeat her.

Her blow caught him in the chest. She took advantage

of the seconds when he was off balance, pulled herself up, then, throwing all her force into her elbow, caught him on the side of the temple. She twisted sideways, pivoted and landed a heel in his solar plexus.

The stunned look in his eyes told her she'd gotten in a good blow and done some damage. She wasn't given time to gloat over her victory, for with the fury of retribution darkening his eyes, he backhanded her, sending her to the floor.

"You should have stayed down. It would have been easier." He picked her up as he would a rag doll and carried her outside, Clariss in his wake.

Dani bit his shoulder. Other than a muttered word, he gave no evidence she'd really hurt him.

Hold on to faith. The words echoed in her mind with increased fervency. *Hold on to faith.*

Dani did just that.

Until she saw the grave.

Freshly dug dirt lay beside the yawning hole in the ground. Cold fear squeezed the breath from her, and she turned pleading eyes to Victor.

"Go ahead. Beg. I'd like to hear it." His laugh was a harsh slash in the night. "Your mother denied me even that."

She wouldn't give him that satisfaction. The breath she struggled to take caught in her throat, searing and terrifying.

Dani called upon every ounce of courage she possessed, though her knees were shaking. At eight, she'd had a severe asthma attack, so bad that she couldn't breathe. She'd felt as if she were being smothered and ever since then had an intense fear of suffocating.

Victor tossed her into the grave, then climbed into a backhoe and fired it up.

Dani's asthma kicked in, winding her. Though she tried to climb out of the grave, she lacked the strength. Dirt cascaded onto her, clogging her nose, stinging her eyes. She struggled to her knees, but the heaping shovels of dirt kept knocking her back down.

Blinking again and again, she worked to clear the grit from her eyes. She shook her head, trying to dislodge the clumps of dirt that clung to her face. "Please, Lord," she prayed. "Help me remain strong."

"Victor, do you have to…?" Clariss's words went unheeded.

Dani rolled onto her stomach to protect her face from the rain of dirt. It didn't help.

The earthen walls seemed to close in around her as the dirt piled on top of her. Darkness. Nightmare. Nothingness.

"How do you know where he's taken her?"

The Jeep sped through the darkening twilight.

"After talking with the senator, I went to the hall of records and found the paperwork where he'd changed his name. I had to go back a long way, but I found it." Grim satisfaction hardened Jake's voice. "It seems Victor Wingate never existed. But a Mick Devane did. He was born not far from Atlanta, in a town called Misty Springs."

"So, why the name change?"

"Mick Devane was born on the wrong side of the tracks. It seems that he always wanted more. So when he came of age, he changed his name. He falsified records to get into Harvard. Wingate even passed the bar and practiced in Massachusetts for a while before returning to Georgia."

"Even when he wanted to erase his roots, he couldn't stay away," Sal mused aloud.

"That's my thinking. You can't deny your roots. Anyway, Mick/Victor settled in Atlanta, fabricated a family background that allowed him to fit into the upper crust of society. He got himself a job at a high-priced firm and joined the movers and shakers. He met Dani at some social event and became fixated on her."

"Can you say *psycho?*" Sal murmured.

Jake nodded. "He's a sociopath. Dani ruined his plan to make her turn to him as she did four years ago. That makes him more dangerous than ever."

"How do you know where he's taken her?" Sal asked again.

"I don't. Not for certain. But I've got a pretty good idea. Hold on." Jake pressed down on the accelerator.

Something called out in his soul at that moment, something deeper than he'd ever experienced before, and he felt God stirring within him.

Dear Lord, please keep Dani safe until I get there. With a start, he realized that, for the first time in over a year, he was praying. The words felt right in his mind, in his heart. How had he ever thought he had given up believing? He'd been only fooling himself.

He'd been fooling himself about Dani, as well. He loved her. It was that simple and that complicated. The idea that he might lose her filled him with such dread that he felt paralyzed. Nothing that had ever happened to him before, nothing that could ever happen in the future would be more devastating than losing her.

They arrived in Misty Springs in less than half the time the drive should have taken. Using the map he'd downloaded from the internet, he followed the directions to the house where Mick Devane had grown up.

The neighborhood where the small frame house stood may have been respectable at one time, but it was clearly on the wrong side of the tracks now. Tufts of grass fought against hard-packed dirt. Apparently the rich fertile soil of Georgia had forgotten this sad piece of land.

Ancient appliances littered the front yard—what there was of it. A picket fence marched drunkenly down the borders of the property. A clothesline drooped between two rusted poles.

More than the hardscrabble poor appearance, though, was the smell of despair that clung to the house. Had it always been so? Jake wondered. Had the house ever burst with energy and happiness? Somehow, he doubted it.

He pulled the Jeep into a rutted lane a short distance from the house and motioned to Sal to proceed quietly. The two men instantly slipped into a routine born of long practice. Jake took point, while Sal flanked him.

They moved silently through the dark where amethyst shadows dimpled the ground in uneven patterns. Evening noises of nocturnal animals making their nighttime appearance were the only sound. The air, heavy with humidity, smelled of wild honeysuckle.

A silver-gray BMW was parked in the front drive. Sal gestured to a compact car parked at its side.

Jake tested the door, found it unlocked. He shone his pen flashlight on the car's registration and wasn't surprised to find that it belonged to Clariss.

He realized the woman had been working with Wingate the entire time. No wonder the letters and packages had been able to be delivered to Dani's office without being detected.

He showed the registration to Sal, who nodded his understanding. In the next moment, Jake spotted Clariss trying to make a run for it. "Get her," he whispered to Sal, who took off after Clariss.

The growl of a backhoe alerted Jake. He ran and stopped when he saw Wingate operating it, systematically covering what appeared to be a freshly dug grave with dirt.

Faint cries cut through the waning light.

Riding on fury, Jake headed to the backhoe. Wingate turned the machine on him, attempting to run Jake over. His Delta training went into high gear. Jake sidestepped and yanked the man from the seat, then aimed a high kick to his chest.

Victor deflected the blow so that Jake's kick only glanced off his shoulder. He grunted but didn't go down. "Is that the best you've got?"

Jake didn't bother with an answer. He swung his leg around, hooking it behind Victor's.

The man stumbled but kept to his feet. He head-butted Jake in the stomach, then reached up to try to gouge his fingers in Jake's eyes. Jake caught Victor by the wrist and bent his arm backward. The bone snapped.

Despite his injuries, Victor sneaked out with his good arm and slammed Jake's head against the side of the back-hoe.

Pain.

Blood.

He forced himself to ignore it. To block everything else out but protecting Dani and himself and defeating the enemy.

Jake shot his fist beneath Victor's nose, sending the man sprawling. Jake didn't give Victor a chance to get up but jumped on top of him, straddling him.

Even with a broken arm, Victor fought with ferocious strength. With a mighty effort, he bucked Jake off.

Twisting, turning, rolling…

Finally, Jake delivered a bone-jarring punch to the man's jaw.

With a wet, gurgling sound, Wingate collapsed. After one futile effort to get up, he stayed down.

Jake yanked him to his feet, handed him over to Sal, who bound his hands with a pair of Flex-Cuffs, having already done the same with a sobbing Clariss. Jake jumped into the would-be grave, dug with his battered hands to uncover the dirt that had piled on top of Dani and pulled her into his arms.

Dani was shaking uncontrollably. Fear and stress had undoubtedly triggered an asthma attack. Holding her as he would something infinitely precious, he lifted her into Sal's arms, then climbed up to kneel beside her.

"I knew you'd come." Her words came in sharp gasps.

He couldn't speak, could only hold her.

"Inhaler," she said, her voice thready. "Cabin."

Gently, he laid her down, brushed the dirt from her, then hurried to retrieve the inhaler and put it to her lips. "Easy does it," he cautioned.

With a few drags on the inhaler, she started to breathe evenly. Jake continued to hold her. He wasn't planning on letting her go anytime soon.

"I'm all right," Dani insisted. With the aid of the inhaler and in the safety of Jake's arms, she was back to her old self. Almost.

"You're still getting checked out at the hospital." Jake's tone brooked no argument.

"Victor." She couldn't repress a shudder that ran through her. Victor had almost succeeded. Had he hated her that much? How had she not seen it? She'd been blind to what he was. Only her mother had seen through the smooth exterior he'd presented to the world.

"Victor's in a pair of cuffs. Monroe's just about to take him in."

"I want to see him."

"Dani." The single word held protest and admiration.

"I have to face him. One more time."

Jake didn't argue with her but motioned to Monroe, who shoved Wingate in their direction.

His face bloodied, arms secured behind his back, Victor was no longer the handsome, charming young lawyer. He lifted his gaze to Dani. "I underestimated you."

Dani stared him down, read the mixture of rage and torment in his gaze. "You overestimated yourself. You know what, Victor? You're going to have to live with yourself for the things you've done." Her voice turned suddenly fierce. "For what you did to my mother. To me. To Clariss. You will live a long, long time in a tiny cell where you get to see daylight for only an hour a day. I'm going to mourn my mother. And then I'm going to live my life. The Lord willing, it will be full and rich and happy." The fire left her voice to be replaced by strength. "And if I ever think of you, I'll try to pray for you. Someday, I may be able to forgive you. But it won't be today."

Victor withered in front of her.

Monroe handed Victor over to a patrolman. "He won't be getting out for a long time. If ever."

"Him and Clariss both," Sal added.

Dani shook her head. "Clariss was a victim as much as I was. She didn't know what he was like. Not really."

"She set you up," Jake reminded her.

"I know. But she can still be saved. I'm going to speak to Freeman about her. Maybe there's something I can do for her."

"You never quit, do you?"

"Not when it matters." Clariss deserved a second chance, and Dani was determined to give it to her. Victor had taken too much already. Dani was not about to allow him to drag someone else into the dark ugliness of his soul.

She submitted to going to the hospital, where she was poked and prodded and pronounced all right.

Under protest, Dani had been convinced to remain at the hospital under observation for the night. Around ten o'clock, she finally gave in to exhaustion.

"She'll probably sleep twelve hours straight," the doctor told Jake and her father. "The best thing you can do for her now is to get some rest yourselves."

The senator turned to Jake. "Thank you, son. You gave me back my daughter. If not for you…" His voice broke.

Jake clasped the older man's arm. "In the end, Dani

saved herself. She kept Wingate talking until we could get to her."

"I'll never be able to thank you and Shelley enough. Be assured that a sizable bonus will be included in your fee."

Right then, Jake wasn't interested in bonuses, sizable or not. Dani was all right. That was all that mattered.

He sensed that the senator wanted time alone with Dani, even though she was asleep. He respected that and left father and daughter alone.

There was something else he wanted to do. He wanted in on the interrogation of Victor Wingate, and when Monroe had invited him, Jake had jumped at the chance.

"Unbelievable," Monroe muttered two hours later, when he, Jake and the D.A. himself had finished the first round of questioning. "The man is certifiably crazy. He's so far gone that he now believes his own lies."

"He's one of the few true sociopaths I've ever encountered," Leonard Freeman said. "Despite what you see on television, real sociopaths are rare."

"As long as he never gets out." Jake didn't care how or what they termed Wingate. He wanted only to make sure the man spent the rest of his days behind bars.

"Misty Springs is in the sheriff's jurisdiction," Monroe said. "They'll let us know when they have identification on the body. But I don't believe there's any question that it's Madeline Barclay."

The grave was next to the open one Wingate had dug for Dani. The memory of that freshly dug grave caused Jake to clench his fists until his knuckles whitened.

They had all agreed that there was no need to notify the senator about finding his wife's body until the identification was certain.

"You want a job on the force?" Monroe asked Jake, only half joking. "You did a bang-up job putting things together."

"I already have a job," Jake reminded him. "And I'd better

make a report to my own boss." It didn't matter that his boss was also his sister. Shelley ran a tight ship and demanded verbal and written reports.

"Go on," the detective said. "I've got a bunch of paper-work to slog through. There's nothing more you can do here tonight." He stuck out a big hand. "It's been a pleasure, Rabb."

"Same goes, Detective." Jake shook hands with the district attorney as well, then headed to his Jeep, where Sal was waiting for him.

"Any chance I can bunk with you tonight?" his friend asked. "I've got to find myself some new digs."

Jake longed for privacy, to sort through his thoughts, but he couldn't refuse his friend. Sal had gone the second mile in protecting Dani. Jake owed him more than he could ever repay.

He started to say just that when Sal stopped him. "We're brothers. Brothers don't need words."

Jake gave him a one-arm hug and headed the Jeep to the house. After the last harrowing hours, bed sounded good. He showed Sal the spare room, then fell into his own bed.

Three hours later, Jake awoke, the scream caught in his throat. His men. Had to reach his men.

He rolled from his bed and groped his way in the darkness, looking for the source of the screams. He put his hands to his ears to block the sound of the cries of his men. *Got to keep moving,* he told himself. *Got to keep moving.* His men needed him.

Meaty hands grabbed him from behind, held him fast.

Jake broke free of the hold, flipped his assailant over and tossed him to the floor.

"Jake! Jake, it's Sal. Wake up, man. You're having a nightmare."

Only then did Jake realize he had his hands around his

friend's throat. "Oh, man. I'm sorry. I'm sorry." His choked words dissolved as shudders overtook his body.

"It's all right," Sal said quietly. "You were having a flash-back. No big deal."

"I could have killed you."

"Nah. You'd have figured it out. Besides, I'm too mean to die."

Sal's reassurance should have settled him. Should have, but didn't.

"Hey. Do you think you're the only one who's ever had a flashback? I've had my share. Still do sometimes." Sal's matter-of-fact acceptance of what had happened helped, but Jake couldn't forgive himself for what he'd done to his friend.

It didn't take a degree in psychiatry to figure out what had triggered the flashback: the nightmare scene at Win-gate's old home. Seeing Dani at the mercy of a madman had somehow gotten mixed up with his own personal misery.

It could have been Dani he'd thrown to the floor. It could have been Dani whom he'd held by the throat, Dani's deli-cate skin he'd bruised. Or worse.

He'd almost lost her to Wingate tonight. Now he had to admit that *he* could be the one to hurt her—or worse. As that picture took shape in his mind, anguish twisted his heart.

He leaned against the bed frame, head in his hands, and for the first time in over a year, he cried. He cried for the men he hadn't been able to save. He cried for Dani, who now had to accept her mother's death. He cried for him-self. He couldn't bring his nightmares into Dani's life, not after what she'd been through. The best thing he could do for her was to get out of her life and stay out.

Sal did him the favor of letting him be. No soldier wanted his friend, his comrade-in-arms, to see him fall apart. It was stupid, but he had to hold on to what little self-respect he had remaining.

Jake stayed where he was, slumped against the side of the bed. He might have dozed for a few minutes. He didn't know.

The following morning, he knew what he had to do. He packed his duffel bag, left a note for Shelley, then climbed into his Jeep and started driving.

He didn't know where he was heading. He didn't much care.

Loneliness.

Ignore it. He couldn't have it all ways. His time with Dani had been comforting, her belief in God a balm to his tortured soul. He had taken from her faith, her strength, but, in the end, he was alone.

Always alone.

TWELVE

Through her office window, Dani watched the sun rise in a glorious, eye-blinding burst of pink and orange over the horizon. She'd arrived at work early, eager to get a head start on the day.

Freedom.

Ever since Victor's arrest, she had held at bay the smothering fear from the threats and ugliness he'd brought into her life, but it had always been there, hovering in the background, waiting to pounce and ambush her. She'd feared lowering her guard for even a moment.

But if she didn't embrace today, with its precious freedom, then Victor would win. She wouldn't allow that.

Several hours later, having made satisfying progress on her caseload, she looked up expectantly when the door to her office swung open.

But it was only the temporary secretary who had been hired until a permanent one could be found. Clariss remained in custody. Dani herself was working on a plea bargain for Clariss in return for turning evidence against Victor.

Dani still believed that, with help, Clariss could be saved. Victor had taken too much already. She wouldn't let him claim Clariss as yet another victim, not if she could help it.

"Ms. Barclay?" The secretary, nearer fifty than forty, looked at Dani. "You have a visitor."

When Shelley Rabb came through the door, Dani immediately rose and embraced her. "Shelley. It's good to see you."

"You may not think so when you hear what I have to say."

Dani's heart constricted. "Jake. Is something wrong?"

"I don't know. I haven't seen or heard from him since the day after Wingate was arrested. He made his report, left me a note saying he was taking some time off, then dropped out of sight."

Dani swallowed. "Have you tried to find him?"

Shelley made an impatient sound. "Of course I tried, but Jake's good. When he doesn't want to be found, he can't be found."

"You've checked with Sal?"

Shelley nodded. "No one's heard a word from him."

Dani sat, gestured for the other woman to do the same. Dani wrapped her arms around her waist, the pain so intense that she feared she would break into pieces. Had she survived what Victor planned for her only to lose the one man she had ever loved, could ever love?

"I'm sorry," Shelley murmured. "You're hurting, and I've only made it worse."

"You told me what you know. I appreciate it." But despair settled on her shoulders, dragging her down, smothering all joy. Even the knowledge that the stalking was over didn't compare to the loss of the man she loved.

"You're in love with him, aren't you?"

Unable to deny it, Dani nodded miserably. She recalled those moments when Jake had held her after rescuing her from the grave where Victor had intended to bury her. He'd cradled her face in his hands, and though his expression was tormented, his gaze had held nothing but tenderness.

"I think Jake feels the same way."

"Then why didn't he try to see me?" The next day, following her release from the hospital, she'd waited for him, all the while allowing herself to dream of a future with him, a future that included picket fences and porch swings, barbecues and family. When a day, then two days, then a week had passed, she'd been worried, then frightened, then angry.

"Jake's carrying around some pretty heavy baggage from his days in the military," Shelley said softly. "I think he's still trying to get a handle on it."

Dani recalled the terrifying nightmare that had made Jake cry out, screaming that he had to get to his men.

"If it's any comfort, he told you a lot more than he did me," Shelley said. "I had to piece together bits of information he'd let slip over the last twelve months."

"Why won't he let me help him?" The words came out on an anguished sob. "I saw him in the middle of a nightmare. I didn't turn away. So why is he turning away from me?" Tears burned Dani's throat, but she swallowed them back. No point in crying. Jake was done with her. He couldn't have made it more plain.

"My guess would be that it tore him apart to let you see him that way. He's not one to show weakness in front of someone else, especially a woman he cares about."

Dani supposed that should have made her feel better. It didn't. "What are we going to do?"

"Wait," Shelley said. "And pray."

"Wait and pray" had become Dani's motto over the past month. Wait, pray and pray some more.

The succeeding weeks took their toll. In the window of the office door, she saw herself reflected, the image gazing back at her confirming what she already knew. Her mouth was pinched, her eyes tired and miserable.

She got through the days because she had no choice.

Patricia Newton's case had gone to trial. The woman had received twelve years for her attempt on Mr. McBride's life. At her boss's directive, Dani had turned the case of the attempted poisoning on herself over to another attorney.

Jerry Brooks had pleaded out, receiving a mandatory sentence of eight years for spousal abuse. Once more, Dani had turned the vandalism case over to another attorney in the D.A.'s office.

Her professional life was on track. She had the respect of her colleagues. Even her father was coming around to accepting that she belonged where she was.

After the funeral for her mother, father and daughter spent time together at Belle Terre. Dani refused to allow herself to dwell on the sense of abandonment she'd felt when Jake had failed to show up for the service. He didn't owe her anything. She'd do well to remember that. Still, betrayal stabbed deep.

On the plus side, her father had returned to church.

"I blamed God when your mother vanished," he said, upon accompanying her to Sunday services for the first time. "No more."

A new closeness grew between them, and Dani rejoiced in it.

"I'm proud of you, darling," her father told her one evening after dinner at Belle Terre. "You survived what would have broken many people."

"I can't help feeling that it's my fault what happened to Mama. I brought Victor into our lives. If I hadn't been dating him, if I'd only listened to her when she tried to warn me against him, things could have been so different." Guilt left a foul taste in her mouth.

He father held up his hand. "None of that. The blame lies on Wingate. He manipulated you. He manipulated all of us. He wormed his way into your life. We'll probably never understand what makes a man like that tick."

"Why didn't I see what he was?" She'd agonized about that over the past weeks, trying to figure out what she could have done differently. She recognized that as part of the healing process, but that acknowledgment didn't take away the pain.

"I think you did. You broke it off with him."

"But I didn't understand how truly twisted he was."

"None of us did." Her father drew her to him. "You're a strong, independent woman, Dani. Your mother would have been proud of you. I know I am."

"Thank you, Daddy."

The senator cleared his throat. "I can't help noticing that I haven't seen Rabb around."

"Jake's gone."

The stark words lashed her heart with stinging stripes. She'd worked to put him from her mind, but that was proving an impossible task. His slow smile replayed itself in her memory.

Jake was in her mind…and her heart…to stay. And she knew there was more healing to be done.

That night, she slipped into bed and hardly noticed that she cried herself to sleep.

Unable to sleep, Jake padded from the bedroom to the porch of the small house he'd rented in the northern part of the state.

The night stretched before him, the darkness threatening to swallow him whole, the long hours before morning tormenting him with memories. Unwillingly, he recalled Dani's quiet understanding when he'd related the details of that last mission to Libya, a mission that still gave him nightmares.

Another picture of Dani flashed through his mind, standing straight and slim at Madeline Barclay's grave. He'd watched as she'd stood slightly apart from her father, as though both daughter and husband needed to absorb their grief separately. She had been pale, fragile, but there was also strength and endurance to her. Only when the coffin had been lowered into the ground had they moved toward each other, embraced.

Jake should have gone to her, let her know that he was

there for her, rather than secretly attending the funeral and then skulking away just as quietly. Self-blame chafed emotions already rubbed raw.

Despite her obvious sorrow, there was a kind of peace on her face, a peace born of faith. He wanted that for himself. It had once been his. He knew what Dani would say: it could be his again. He had only to claim it.

Light seeped into the sky. He packed the few belongings he'd taken with him and loaded his Jeep. The weeks alone had been cathartic, as had revisiting the families of his fallen comrades. He'd gone to see them after returning to the States, as a kind of penance.

This visit had been different, as he'd shared stories of husbands and fathers, sons and brothers. The families had been pathetically eager for any scrap he could provide. No one blamed him for what had happened. So why did he still blame himself? Maybe it was time to start facing life instead of running from it. That was what the shrink he'd started seeing again had told him.

"I know you're a man of faith," the doctor had said. "Part of faith is forgiveness. Maybe it's time you started forgiving yourself."

"I don't know if I can."

"Ask the Lord. He knows our hearts, and His love is big enough for all of us."

The doctor had been right. It was Jake's first step in recovery, asking for the Lord's help in forgiving himself. With that as a base, he could start to forgive others.

As he pulled out of the driveway, he acknowledged that he'd run out of excuses to avoid returning to Atlanta. To Dani.

He wouldn't blame her if she wanted nothing to do with him. He'd walked out on her with no word, no explanation. She deserved better than that, especially after what she'd been through.

Depending on someone, anyone, went against his nature, but he needed Dani in a way he'd never needed anyone. If she turned him away, he wouldn't know what to do.

He found Shelley at her office. "Shell?"

She looked up from her laptop, glared at him, looking like a small wet hen who'd had her feathers ruffled. "It's about time, big brother."

He didn't waste time on preliminaries. "How is she?"

Shelley didn't pretend to misunderstand. "Lonely. Hurting."

"Because of me."

His sister didn't spare him and nodded. "Because of you."

"I love her." He said the words with a kind of awe. Until then, he'd believed love was lost to him forever. Now he knew it wasn't lost; it had been only misplaced.

With all its twists and turns, ups and downs, love had triumphed. It was back. His heart was full with it. For Dani.

"I know."

"I don't know if she'll have me." The words were the hardest he'd ever said.

"You won't know until you ask. If you love her, fight for her." Shelley laid a hand on his arm. "You've never run from a fight in your life. I don't expect you to start now."

The unsympathetic words were just what he needed.

"Go to her. Tell her what you told me." She paused, deliberately. "Or let her go."

"I don't have the right to ask her to share my life. I'm broken inside."

"We're all broken somehow. You have a head start on the rest of us. You recognize that you need help and you're getting it." She threw him a challenging look. "If you'd get out of your own way, you'd probably figure out that she's in love with you, too."

Did Dani feel that way? He wasn't so sure. He didn't know if he had the right to ask her to let him back into her life. But Shelley was right about one thing. He had two choices. Go to Dani or walk away from her. Forever.

In the end, he did what he'd known he had to: he went to Dani. He found her at her desk, nose buried in a book that looked as if it weighed more than she did. Content to watch her, to absorb the essence that was Dani, he didn't speak.

Then, as if sensing his presence, she looked up. Her eyes widened, then went blank of all expression. "Jake."

"Yeah."

"I didn't expect to see you."

"I didn't expect to see myself here." He searched for the right words and found only the truth. "I hurt you."

The answer in her eyes was painful to see, a confirmation of the guilt he'd been carrying for the past month.

"I'm not expecting sympathy."

"Good. Because you're not getting any." She lifted her chin, stared at him, daring him to contradict her.

It was such a familiar gesture that he smiled. The smile died as quickly as it took shape.

"Why, Jake? Why did you leave? I needed you." Unshed tears turned her voice husky. "I needed you at my mother's funeral."

"I was there," he said.

"You were?" At his nod, she asked, "Why didn't you say something?"

"I was afraid."

"Afraid of what?"

"Of hurting you more than I already had." He wet his lips and took the biggest risk of his life. Dani deserved to know the truth. "I didn't want to leave you. That night when you were in the hospital, I had another nightmare. Sal was unlucky enough to get in my way. I almost choked him."

"But you didn't."

"No. I didn't. But only because Sal was quicker than I was and took me down. What if it had been you, Dani?

What if it were your throat I had my hands around? If I hurt you…I couldn't go on living. I wouldn't want to go on living."

"You would never hurt me." Her voice held unmistakable certainty.

At her words, something like hope built in his heart. "You saw me when I was caught in a nightmare. You know what it's like. I don't know what I'm doing. Or—" he paused "—who I'm going to hurt."

"I survived." She framed his face with her hands. "You saved me, Jake. Now it's my turn to save you." With infinite gentleness, she pressed a kiss to his lips. "I know what guilt feels like. I've been fighting my own nightmares over bringing Victor into my family's life."

That encouraged him to share the guilt that had plagued him for over a year. "If I'd paid attention to what my gut was telling me, I'd have scrubbed the mission. Instead, I listened to the brass and followed orders. And seven men paid the price for my mistake."

"You weren't to blame. Any more than I was to blame for what Victor did." Her voice trembled, then steadied. "I finally did what I should have done in the first place."

"What's that?"

"I turned it over to the Lord. I told him that if He saw fit to help me understand, then I was ready, but that I couldn't do it by myself."

"That's the key, isn't it?" he mused. "Turning it over to the Lord and allowing Him to do the heavy lifting." Hearing himself say it aloud eased much of the pain that had twisted inside his stomach and sent poisonous barbs to his heart over the past year.

"I don't know why God didn't save my mother any more than I know why He didn't save your men. I wish I did," Dani said. "But that's not for me—or you—to figure out.

Our job is to go on living, to try and make a difference in this crazy world."

"That's what the shrink said."

"Sounds like a pretty smart doctor."

"He is." Jake laid a hand over hers. "But it doesn't change the fact that I've got plenty of work to do before I even approach normal. Why would you want to tie your life to a broken-down soldier who lives with nightmares?"

"Because I love him with all my heart." She wrapped her arms around his neck and hugged him. He felt her heartbeat, strong and sure, against his chest. "With God, all things are possible," she said, voice soft as a prayer.

That was like Dani, looking to the Lord for a solution. With her help, maybe he could find his way back to doing the same. "I don't deserve you."

The smile she turned on him was brilliant and so full of joy that it took his breath away. "How about letting me decide that?" She linked her fingers with his and kissed him lightly. "Whatever we face, we face together."

Together. What a beautiful word. Why had he never realized that? He and Dani had a lifetime of togetherness. He could hardly wait to start.

* * * * *

Dear Reader,

I have always stood in awe of the valiant men and women who serve our country in the armed services. Some come home broken in body, others broken in spirit. The idea of a broken hero intrigued me.

With that in mind, I drew Jake Rabb, an ex-Delta soldier, returning from the Middle East and still dealing with the nightmares from that time. The heroine, Dani Barclay, is broken as well, grieving over the disappearance of her mother. Two broken people, looking for love but afraid to reach for it.

I hope you find in Jake and Dani's story a reminder that love, especially with the Lord's tender mercies, can heal the most wounded soul.

Jane M. Choate

Questions for Discussion

1. Do you think Dani made the right choice in refusing to run back to her father and allow him to protect her with all of the resources at his command?

2. Do you believe Jake was too harsh in his initial judgment of Dani as a "spoiled princess"? Have you ever made similar judgments and then later regretted them?

3. Do you think that all judgments are bad or do you believe that making some judgments is a necessary part of life?

4. Have you ever grieved over something in the past that appeared to have no answer, such as the disappearance of Dani's mother? If so, how have you handled it?

5. Do you agree with Dani's decision to refuse to trade leniency in Patricia Newton's case for information that could help identify the stalker?

6. Was Dani being stubborn in insisting upon attending the awards night, at the risk of her own safety, or was she simply trying to fulfill a promise she'd made? What would you have done in a similar situation?

7. Do you think Dani was foolish in wanting to help Clariss even after all that Clariss had done to betray Dani?

8. Near the end of the book, did you think Jake was selfish in leaving Dani after his nightmare?

9. Would you have forgiven Jake as Dani did? Or would you see his behavior as abandonment? Does forgiveness mean condoning?

COMING NEXT MONTH FROM
Love Inspired® Suspense

Available November 4, 2014

DEADLY HOLIDAY REUNION
by Lenora Worth

Jake Cavanaugh's daughter has been kidnapped by a serial killer, and the only person he can turn to for help is Ella Terrell, a former FBI agent...and his old high school sweetheart.

HAZARDOUS HOMECOMING
Wings of Danger • by Dana Mentink

A found necklace reopens an old missing persons case and changes everything for Ruby Hudson and Cooper Stokes. They must put the past behind them in order to find the truth before someone silences them.

TWIN THREAT CHRISTMAS
by Rachelle McCalla

Long-lost twin sisters have a chance to reunite at Christmastime if they can stay alive long enough to find each other.

SILENT NIGHT STANDOFF
First Responders • by Susan Sleeman

The last person Skyler Brennan wants to spend Christmas Eve with is her FBI agent ex-boyfriend, but she'll have to trust him with her life—and heart—when a bank robber comes after her seeking revenge.

IDENTITY WITHHELD
by Sandra Orchard

A widowed firefighter is determined to rescue a woman in witness protection from her pursuers. But when the criminals involve his son, will he be able to save them both?

PERILOUS REFUGE
by Kathleen Tailer

After witnessing a murder, Chelsea Rogers goes on the run. Can she trust Alex Sullivan to protect her from the killer on her trail—before she becomes the next victim?

LISCNM1014